Big River's Daughter

BOBBI MILLER

Holiday House / New York

Library of Congress Cataloging-in-Publication Data
Miller, Bobbi.
Big River's Daughter / by Bobbi Miller. — 1st ed.
p. cm.
Summary: When River Fillian's powerful father, a pirate
on a Mississippi keeler, disappears after a horrific earthquake in 1811,
she must challenge the infamous rivals who hope to claim his territory and
find her own place in the new order. Includes historical notes.
Includes bibliographical references.
ISBN 978-0-8234-2752-9 (hardcover)
[1. River boats—Fiction.   2. Pirates—Fiction.   3. Adventure and adventurers—Fiction.
4. Christmas, Annie (Legendary character)—Fiction.   5. Laffite, Jean—Fiction.
6. Fink, Mike, 1770–1823?—Fiction.   7. Buried treasure—Fiction.
8. New Madrid Earthquakes, 1811–1812—Fiction.
9. Mississippi River—History—19th century—Fiction.]
I. Title.
PZ7.M61234Big 2013
[Fic]'—dc23
2012033733

For Eric: Glorious Guru, Friend, Fellow Pirate:
"Now and then we had a hope that if we lived and
were good, God would permit us to be pirates."
—Mark Twain, *Life on the Mississippi*

Acknowledgments

Thank you to Eric Kimmel, master guru, for his guidance and inspiration, and for his books on the pirates Laffite and the river outlaws, and for his insights into the French language! *Merci!* To Kitty Tomlinson Wood, wonderful librarian of the Iberville Parish Library, Louisiana, for her invaluable expertise and help with research. To Garth Wells and Jenny Tobin of the Maine Windjammer Association, captains of the *Lewis R. French* of Camden, Maine, a National Historic Landmark and the oldest active commercial schooner, for answering all my questions on sailing. To Karen Grencik, literary agent extraordinaire and friend, for her unwavering support. To Emma D. Dryden, founder and proprietor of drydenbks, and also—with much affection—the wise Dumbledore who kept me focused on the right journey. To Jill Santopolo, and my fellow writing students in her class, who offered reviews and insights as I was beginning to create River's journey. And to Pam Glauber, my most fabulous editor, for her steadfast support and insightful observations that helped bring life to River and her friends.

Introduction

On December 16, 1811, the central Mississippi Valley was rocked by an earthquake. This quake registered at magnitude 8 by current standards, making it stronger than the earthquake that leveled San Francisco in 1906. It was so strong, its effects were felt as far as Boston, a thousand miles away, where bells tolled because of the shaking. Damage was reported as far away as Washington, DC. It was so strong, it turned the waters of the Mississippi River. December 16 became known as the day the Mississippi River ran backward.

This here story is all true, as near as I can recollect. It ain't a prettified story. Life as a river rat is stomping hard, and don't I know it. It's life wild and woolly, a real rough and tumble. But like Da said, life on the big river is full of possible imaginations. And we river rats, we aim to see it through in our own way. That's the honest truth of it.

—River Fillian

Part One

December
1811

Chapter One

The Mississip. She moves slow, this big river, like cold sorghum. But there's power in each ripple. It's like muscles on a puma ready to pounce. I watch as she moves.

The air is heavy with heat and haze. Something's astir. Da feels it and looks down at me. He once told me, he counted just three moments that mattered in his life. He met Ma the same day he met the big river, and he says in that moment, both took hold of his blood like an undertow. The rest of his life, he ain't never let go of either.

For a few years he rode the river while Ma made a home in a small shoreline town. But soon enough, in a moment like the quiet flicker of light shifting on the river, Ma passed. Same day he said good-bye to Ma, Da met me. I came into this world with a thunderclap. And in that moment, he says, he met his angel.

Me, an angel?

When I was new born, Da brought me on board. Them other keelers thought me a bad omen. Women and children don't belong on a boat, they said. A girl-child is double cursed. A girl on board, they said, makes the river angry. But then, I was born during a rough-and-tumble storm, born knowing the Mississip. I'm their anchor, says Da. So they called me River.

"What do you see, little River?" Da asks me.

"Can't see a dang thing through that haze, Da." I wag my head and try harder.

"That's the thing." He crouches like a lion now. "It's the haze itself. It ain't right."

Da was once a civilized man, a real highborn son from Virginia. He was learning to be a lawyer, just like his da. GrandDa was a respectable lawyer, I expect, believing in fairness for all. After the war GrandDa defended a Tory accused of murdering some patriot. Seems like them patriots didn't want to hear any talk but their own. They had already determined the man was guilty.

One night them patriots came to GrandDa's home. They threatened to tar and feather him but good if he didn't change his thinking. But GrandDa said civilized men should be able to talk about such matters and come to some agreement. Them patriots beat him plenty. When Da came to help him, they beat him, too. Then they shaved both their heads, stripped them to their britches, and dabbed hot tar over their heads, chests, and arms. But the tar was too hot, and GrandDa died screaming.

But that ain't the worse of it. Them patriots burned his house. It burned too fast, killing Da's ma and his sister. That day Da lost his whole family. So he ran away—left the civilized life and found his way to the Mississip. Da carries the scar of that day across his cheek.

Da smiles, one of them weak, hiding smiles.

"It's a-comin'," he whispers, but everyone on the boat hears him. I can see them wagging their heads in worry, looking to the sky. They can't see it, what's coming, but they trust Da. If he says something's astir, they know it's the honest truth.

Da turns back to the bow. His eye follows the swelling river. "Gurdy! Wind that horn again!"

Gurdy, the first mate, blows into the horn, a soft, sad sound that floats into the fog. Even before the note falls away, the second keeler picks it up.

In all my born years, I ain't ever heard Da so afeared. It sends my own hackles rising. He combs his fingers through his shock of orange hair and then smoothes his chin hairs. His blue eyes turn gray when he's in a worm of worry. Now they are as deep a gray as the fog.

"What's it mean, Da?"

"Can't figure it out." He stares so hard into the haze, his eyes might slice right through the thick of it. He ain't near as big as most men on his three boats, but he carries himself tall.

Ain't no man knows the river like Daniel Fillian. Da knows her like a lawyer knows his books—every sandbar, curve, and wayward island in the long stretch of the muddiest, crookedest river, always shifting her ways. But that ain't why they call him king of the river. That's not why the men listen to him when he smells something wrong. They follow because he can outtalk, outfight, and outsmart any other keeler. He outsmarts most men in general, even that rioting rascal Mike Fink.

Da stands right up and booms, "All right, mannies, stand to your poles!"

There's no dawdling when Da commands. Not even by me, despite once or twice me giving it a good try. I jump atop the cabin. That's my post, using Da's spyglass. And there ain't nothing like this spy case. Da made it special, long before I came along. He carved it from oak, fitted it with gold bands, and carved out birds and dragons around it. It's a beaut. He made the spyglass, too, and ain't it some. Real shiny. He taught me to use the spyglass to read the shores and the stars to see our way around the river. Ain't ever had a need for books or proper learning. But he taught me to read the river, all right.

I look shore to shore to see what follows. I look across the river's surface to see what might be bubbling up.

But now I can't see nothing through this unnatural haze. It even smells different, heavy with wet and earth and . . . something else . . . something rotting.

I can hear the steersmen on the other two boats echo Da's warning. On all three boats, men jump on the runway, their stomping echoes down the line like drumbeats. Everyone stands on dog alert.

Da stands on the prow of his keeler *Molly Dear*. This keel's named for Ma, and a fine beaut she is. From bow to stern, she's fifty feet. Her cabin stands in the middle of the deck, with a tall mast for sails. Working upriver, life becomes all toil and danger. It requires a man's blood and muscle to pull her against the current.

But who-op, going downriver when the wind is with us, we set sail. And then we see life uncivilized, life in its glory, says Da. The two other keelers in Da's flotilla—the *Lady Twilight* and *Little Fanny*—are not as large as the *Molly Dear* but just as stout. And the three of them sailing down the big river is a sight to behold.

Da stands on the prow. That's how he likes it, especially when his hackles are raised. Whatever comes his way, he means to charge it head-on, like a bull. He's looking fierce, all right.

Suddenly, Curt roars from the second boat, "Set poles!"

I hear each man stomping on the sweep so fast, it's a whirr of thunder.

Then Curt roars again. "Throw your poles wide, boyos! Brace off!"

Using the spyglass, I peer at the river's ripples, trying to see my way below the surface.

"Starboard!" I point to a huge rotting black tree bouncing on the current, its roots still planted in the river.

"Heave into it!" Curt booms, twisting the helm. The poles-men stab their pole ends into the tree. "That's it, mannies, put your backs into it!" Curt booms. "Push as if your life depends on it!"

"Wagh!" Each man roars his challenge to the river. The boat groans as it edges into a turn.

Branches scrape against the running boards, and I can feel the wood-on-wood grind in my very teeth. But the boat clears the tree and eases into smoother water.

"Who-op!" Curt roars again. "Now ain't that happifying!"

And others join him with some big fancy stomping on deck.

"He did it, Da!" I dance atop the cabin. "Curt can steer a boat floating on dew!"

But Da just wags his head, turning back to the river ahead. Already Da knows his next move. "River, fetch me three of them rounders."

In two leaps I'm off the cabin roof. Strapping the spyglass in its case against my back, I bolt inside to grab the bucket of stones. Choosing three big rounders, I take them to Da.

He bounces one in his palm, even as he studies the water ahead. He whispers, "Get ready."

I nod. I know that look: I'm going ashore.

I swerve about and untie the skiff, a small, flat-bottom row-boat with a pointed bow and a flat stern.

Swinging his arm back, Da throws the rock straight ahead. It disappears into the haze, then splashes loud as it hits the water. Da twitches, looking deeper into the haze, changing directions. He throws another rock. A moment later, it splashes.

"You ready, River?" he looks down at me.

"Always," I straighten my shoulders. He throws this third rounder and cocks his ear. This time, the water sounds hollow as the rock hits the shallows.

"Round to, River," he booms. "Land ho! Not more than fif-teen feet. I'm right behind you!"

I'm already gathering the rope. With a nod to Da, Gurdy drops the coiled rope into the skiff. I make sure it's secured on the deck.

I jump into the skiff first and make my way to the bow. With a heave Gurdy follows me aboard, easing near the stern. He clenches a long blade between his teeth. That's Big Sally, his best gal, he says. Big enough to slice through anything that slithers our way.

Me at the bow, and Gurdy at the stern, we row into the haze, toward shore.

"Look sharp, little River," he says. Next to Da, Gurdy knows the river best. Gurdy's father was a Creek, born on the Missis-sip. His ma was a slave woman who escaped from the riots in Santo Domingo. Once a slave himself, now he's a river man. He's Da's first mate and truest friend. And next to Da he's my truest friend, too.

Gurdy's face is brown as old parchment, his dark eyes always ashine. He's a stocky barrel. His curly, untamed hair looks like

9

a halo. Most days it flies loose around his head. Some days, like this day, he wears a red bandana to tame it some. He has just as much hair on his chin, and most often, it's just as untamed. But today he's braided it with a red ribbon.

It's hard rowing. The river swells push us aside, away from the shore.

"She's fit to be tied, Gurdy." I study the swirls. "Being pure stubborn."

"Nothing you can't handle," Gurdy says.

Together Gurdy and me push and pull the oars until we come in-line with the shore, easing closer with every row.

I can hear it now, the water slapping the riverbank. Jumping out of the boat, I'm waist-deep in the big river. My toes brush the muddy bottom. The water's cold, right to the bone.

"Who-op!" I yodel, signaling Da that we made it ashore. I grip the front of the skiff, and Gurdy takes the side.

"Heave to, little River!" Gurdy says. We pull it higher onto dry land.

"That's my wee angel!" Da yodels back.

The river's not yet chewed this bank to a nib. Willows and oak still grow mightily tall not far off the waterline. Gurdy takes up the slack in the rope, wraps it quick about one of them sturdy trunks, and pulls it tight.

"Who-op!" I yodel again. An echo later, Da returns the call. He's drifting the keeler to point inland. I can hear big oars slapping the river, moving the boat closer. The *Molly Dear* oozes out of the haze as it follows the line.

And there stands Da on her prow. Something still ain't right though. I can tell from his stance and the way he's looking at the sky.

Only now can I see outlines of other boats moored in this stretch of land. How many others are seeking refuge from this haze?

The very air is atingle. Not a bird trills, nor an insect buzzes about our necks. Not a sound comes out of them woods.

Something terrible, something really terrible is astir.

Chapter Two

The heavens open up all at once, and rain pours down in sheets with cracks of thunder. The wind begins to chase us as we fly through the woods, Da leading the way. I keep at his heels, swatting aside branches and brush. Gurdy's on my shadow, pushing me along.

"Get your wiggle on, River," Da shouts above the thunder. "Almost there, mannies. Step to it!"

The lightning spreads over everything. An eerie, warm rain soaks us through despite it being dead winter.

Another flash, and a bellow of thunder. I shudder, adjusting the case strapped to my back, making sure the spyglass is snug.

As the woods pull apart I recognize where we are. I've been here before. I can hear music cut through the rain. It's honey on my biscuits, and I smile. Someone's waxing on a fiddle, and another trying to keep up with a banjo.

"Careful now! Hear tell this island is thick with pirates!" Da shouts, but the men don't need encouraging. They hoot and yodel. Gurdy throws me up over his shoulders and runs like a hungry chicken through the woods.

Another turn and we reach the blockhouse, a massive square building two stories high. Loopholes, them windows that are no more than narrow slits in the wall, huddle on the second floor. There in front is the only way in and out, a burly door as massive as the timbered walls. The militia long ago abandoned them earthworks and timbers. But we river rats who know the particular usefulness of the blockhouse's location did not forget;

it's a faraway place, beyond the watchful eye of a governor or a constable.

Da raises a fist, signaling us to stop our advance. He draws his pistol from his belt. The others take his lead. Gurdy eases me onto the ground, taking out Big Sally. Da looks to me with a sly, knowing grin. "You stay put until we know it's safe. I hear pirates are afoot!"

He chuckles and winks. Because don't I know, ain't no pirates here like us!

He leads the way inside the fort. Charging through the door, he fires his pistol. Gurdy follows. Not one to stay put, I shadow them both. All heads snap our way. Benches scrape across the floor as some stand up slow, full of menace. Some are even growling.

But not a one is moving.

It's a cavernous room, dark and smoky, heavy with the smells of coal fire and rushlight and a fire crackling in the center pit. I can see all them faces looking at us. Some are pitted with anger, and some are scarred from living a hard life. Some are aged with deep crevices.

But not one face do I know.

Standing there, I smile, too. Ain't nothing here to be afeared of, except my da.

In one far corner stands a banjo player atop one table. He's tall and bent as a sapling. A fiddler stands nearby, not quite as tall, but just as bent. They're both oak stiff, their hands stopped midplay of a melody.

Above, chickens roosting in the rafters are clucking heap-a-plenty.

The second floor is not but a few planks rimming the walls, close to the loopholes. They're situated high, and close to the ceiling, so those inside can watch for anyone coming. But there's no one on watch.

We've taken them all by surprise.

The loudest noises are the crackling of the logs in the center pit and the rain beating down on the timbers.

Da pushes me behind him. Gurdy tries to do the same. I wiggle my way out, but I stay quiet.

"You!" an oily voice booms. A burly man oozes out of the flickering shadows. He pulls from his belt a large pointed dagger, almost as big as Big Sally. Gurdy growls and steps forward, Big Sally in hand. Da holds a hand up, and Gurdy stops. Then Da turns about, smiling fierce. The man shouts again. "Best be telling me how you come to these parts, and convince me why I shouldn't be giving you a good hiding!"

Da grins, his jaw stiffens, his shoulders straighten. He moves forward like a puma, each step deliberate.

Men rush from the tables. Some jump atop the tables, all scrambling to get out of the way.

"Who's this little manny dares crack my lice?" Da booms. "Best get your kickers out of the way, or I'll be the one to give you a severe licking!"

"Who-op!" The man steps forward, puffing himself up. "Who's *this*, say you? This"—his dagger floats through the air—"this is Plug Tyler! I'm the reg'lar screamer chock-full of fight. And I'm a-warning you to say your prayers."

Da's grin crackles like the fire as he plucks out his own big blade. "Well, Plug Tyler, I'm a poor man, true enough. I have been told I smelled like a wet dog. But I'm a tough ole snapping turtle with gator's teeth. And I can whip any man on the Mississip."

"Who-op!" Gurdy echoes Da's challenge, raising Big Sally. "He be the king of this river!"

That's my da. The pirate king!

"Who-op!" Curt and the others carry the thunder.

They're all a-spoiling for a fight, and Da is going to give them one.

The banjo player stomps his foot and strums his own challenge. His grin is as crooked as the river. It's enough to get my goat to see him stomping there.

I crow as loud as any of them. I mean to put that fiddling dog in his place. I quickstep around the room, easing up sideways to the fiddler unnoticed.

Here's a streak of lightning you ain't count on. I'm a mere yearling, but I was born on the river wild! And I can surely outfiddle you!

And just like that, I pinch the fiddle right from his hands. I crow again, racing across the room cat-quick, out of harm's way.

"Well, looky here." Da now strolls around the room, looking into the eye of every man there. "I'm that ring-tail roarer, boyo, that streak of lightning who can outrun, outjump, outshoot any man from St. Louie to New Orleans. Come on, any of you flatters, see how tough I am to chew!"

I jump atop a table, and now I make that fiddle sing.

Plug Tyler throws me a glance, full of menace.

Now Da circles Plug. "Who is *this*, little manny? Surely you heard of me? I towed a tornado cross the Big Muddy with my teeth and broke snags so thick, a fish couldn't swim underneath without rubbing off his scales!"

The banjo player twangs out a melody. I fire up the fiddle to match his song. The banjo player's fingers dance like spitfire. But he can't hold me down any more than that Plug Tyler can take my da!

Da sashays in a wide circle now, himself coiling like a snake ready to strike. Just then a shot rings out, and a new voice thunders.

The stomping stops.

The banjo stops.

Da stops his dancing, and I stop the fiddling. For sure, the chickens stop clucking and even the rain stops falling.

The circle of men pull apart, and there . . . there . . .

She floats across the floor as a swan glides on water. With a long neck and square shoulders, she stands six feet six if an inch. She towers easy over Da, and most men in the room. Her skin shines like the midnight sky. Braids run the length of her back, bundled together with cloth the color of twilight, the same color as her trousers.

"Hate to spoil your pretty dance." She grins, and then she roars, "I tamed that lightning with a smile, riding up the river on that gator's back, leaving you little mannies in my wake! I can sure as spit whip every man here, ten with one hand and twenty with another." She walks around the room looking at every man eye to eye. "I ain't had a real fight in a week and I'm right spoilin' for a good one, here and now. I'm needing more pearls to add to my collection."

And that's when I see them, the string of pearls wrapping twice about the big woman's neck. She glares around the room with cat-green eyes. Not a man stirs; all are afeared of that gaze.

Not even Da moves. But he smiles, and scratches his chin, and wags his head. "Annie Christmas."

"Tenderfoot." She returns his grin. "I see your young'un grows fast." She winks at me.

"Like a rabbit ready to run," says Da. "She cut her teeth on a paddle seasoned with Mississip mud. Full of spit and vinegar, just like her da."

Annie Christmas throws a glance behind her, and up saunter five men. One man saunters up to Plug, his grin as sharp as a dagger.

Plug swallows, his who-op gone.

And Da chuckles. "And I see your little mannies have grown some. How long has it been?"

"Too long." Annie nods, smiling with a mother's pride. "You recognize Cam, my eldest. That there tall black oak is Crow. And them my younger twins, Cay and Cane. And my youngest there with the pearly whites be my Cully. Left their five brothers with the boat."

I ain't ever seen a man so tall as that Crow, him the color of a crow's feathers. And Cam, as burly as two bulls snorting fire, scowling downright fearsome. And them twins, Cay and Cane, the very reflection of each other, like looking into calm waters and seeing yourself stare back. And Cully smiles pretty, green eyes flashing mischief.

As Annie turns about, gliding across the floor, I expect not even the devil dare step up for a rough-and-tumble with them.

Annie smiles, showing her own full set of teeth.

"Is there no one of you wee creatures to take up my challenge? I say, I do so need another pearl."

Da chuckles again. "This damnable thunder and rain sent us all a-hiding. Just make the best of it." Then he points to me with a wink and shouts, "Music!"

Once again I fire up the fiddle. The banjo player stomps, nods his head, and don't you know, he smiles pretty now.

"I say we all have a drink!" Da booms again. "On Plug Tyler!"

And the hall lifts up a hail. Plug spits, not at all pleased. But soon enough even Plug cracks a grin, knowing well enough the best man won.

"And give a hail to the king of them river pirates!" Plug roars.

The Mississip is a roving place, a dangerous place these days. The Spanish, the English, and the French all lay claim to her shores. All wrath converges on these river islands, as pirate, highwayman, and statesman alike all look for his piece of gold. But the Mississip, she's one tough lady and don't take to everyone.

I ain't ever seen this many gather under one roof. Anywhere else, we might be fighting bloody with each other. But the eerie rain had sent us all inside a safe haven. The air is still heavy, and the thunder cracks with a warning. It's still coming, this terrible something.

But here inside the pirates' den, the music's a-playing, the fire's a-cracking, and some chickens are cooking on the spit. It's life on the raggedy edge. Who-op!

Chapter Three

"One of these days, Annie Christmas, they'll be telling stories about you." Despite Da's grin the vein across his forehead bulges as he squares off with Annie. Their hands are gripping—steel against steel—his elbow firmly planted on the table.

Annie puffs her cigar and blows a perfect ring. It hovers over her head like a halo. She winks at me. "They already do, Tenderfoot. Told a few of the better ones myself."

Glowing bright as their cigars are lighted dried piths from rush stalks soaked in fat. There the two sit, just like that, for one hour passing and a second hour almost done. Da grinning and Annie blowing them smoke rings, waiting for the rain to ease, their arms locked in a vise grip. The thunder still rumbles, but not near as loud as those men snoring in the corners. Gurdy's slumped over asleep near the door. Curt and his crew take up the floor near the fire. Annie's boys are slumped on the upper floor. Even them chickens asleep in their roost are snoring up a storm.

It's just us three: Da, Annie, and me.

I sit close to Da, head resting on my arms. I try to sleep, but the thunder and the snoring keep me awake. That, and the sparkle of them pearls wrapped around Annie Christmas's neck.

Da grins at me. "When your da and Miss Annie here first met, that necklace was not so full-grown."

Annie brushes one of her long pointed fingers across them near-perfect round pearls, all a-shiny like the full-bright moon. Even in the dim glow of rushlight, I can see them ain't ordinary pearls. Some are aglow with pink and the colors of twilight. Others are soft with the colors of the sea. But one pearl—twice the size of rest and black as the deepest moonless night—hangs square in the middle.

"That be my first pearl, little River." Annie nods toward me. "Courtesy of another screamer who thought himself king of the river."

"Mike Fink." I chuckle.

"Mike Fink, indeed. You're looking at the only one ever to beat that rascal. If you believe the stories." Da leans into his arm.

I always knew they were longtime friends, Da and Annie Christmas. All my life I heard tell the adventures of Annie Christmas and her boyos. Never thought them stories were more than fancified fairy tales. Any man loses a fight with Annie owes her a pearl. Her boyos make sure the fool man pays his debt. Heard tell, ain't a man alive can beat Annie Christmas, any more, Da says, than one can swim against the big river. The river always wins. Annie Christmas always wins. That's why they call her the Big River's Daughter. And her keeler, *Big River's Daughter,* is the best keeler on the Mississip.

Come to think of it, I wonder if one of them pearls was gift from Da.

Annie puffs another ring and smiles all the more. "I known your da for a long while, since he first came to these parts. Since before your ma, bless her soul, and since before you were a twinkle in his eye. That da of yours is some, true enough. A good man with a golden heart. Too golden to be a pirate, you ask me."

"No sweet talking, now." Da's grin is pretty stiff. "I ain't letting go."

Annie puffs another ring, and sends it dancing circles around my head. She ain't even breaking a sweat. "This here second pearl, tinged with twilight, this one's courtesy of your da."

"Ain't that some." Now I find it hard to stop grinning, and Da throws me one prickly look.

"Don't need you teaching my girl your sass, Annie Christmas," Da snorts.

"Don't think your daughter needs any teaching in that area," says Annie.

Annie scratches her chin, and I wonder if this match will ever see its end. Then Annie's face grows long, and she speaks in mere whispers. "Heard tell Little Harpe is ghosting these parts."

"Not what I heard." Now Da loses his grin. But he keeps his grip—and his eye—on Annie. Even I know this story. Way back when the English and the Spanish and the French were battling over who owns this piece of river, Samuel Mason and Little Harpe were a-robbing and murdering folk all along these parts. Mason collected himself some powerful treasure. He lived mightier and higher than King George himself. When the French finally caught up with him, he had safely hidden his cache. But that weasel Little Harpe helped Mason escape the French, then murdered him in his sleep. He sent his head back to the French to collect the bounty. Then Little Harpe disappeared with Mason's treasure.

Da tightens his grip. Annie tightens her grip, too. I wring my own fingers at the sight of it. Then says she, her whisper more like a rumble, "But there's more to that tale, Tenderfoot. That ain't just any treasure. Heard tell Mason found it. Blackbeard's gold. That's what the French were after. That's what that murdering weasel stole from Mason. And now the Spanish are after Little Harpe."

Blackbeard's treasure? I bolt straight up, looking at Da. He don't offer a twitch or a blink to Annie's tale. But ain't this an interesting turn! Tales have long been told about that rapscallion, that old Edward Teach, the grisliest pirate, who once wrestled with Charleston's highborns. After that, he moved to live the high life in North Carolina till he got bored with it, then he went down in a hail of musket balls almost one hundred years past! Heard tell, he had himself a chest of Spanish silver and French gold and English jewels.

"Fairy tales, Annie?" says Da. Da's fingers and forearm tremble, sweat beading on his temple. "For a hundred years they've been digging up every beach, every island, and every coastal inlet from Barbados to Boston. Ain't no treasure to be found." He inhales sharp, loosens his grip, and blinks. It's just a tick in time, but it's long enough. He's lost this match, and he knows it.

Snake-quick, Annie twists her wrist and slams Da's arm down. "Who-op! That's another match I win, and you owe me another pearl, Tenderfoot. Make it a dandy, sure enough."

I let loose such a laugh, there's no taming it now.

"Didn't think you one to play with the truth just to win a pearl." Da shakes his fingers and rubs his forearm as he scowls at me.

"Hell's bells," Annie puffs. "There's no cheatin' in fighting the rough-and-tumble. The best woman always takes the day. Besides, have you ever known me to joke about silver and gold?"

Da leans in closer still. He looks to me before turning to Annie. His grin is sharp as he scratches his chin. "And you know about Mason finding Blackbeard's treasure because you have a storybook with a treasure map?"

"A treasure map, Tenderfoot? What child's tomfoolery is that?" Annie rolls her eyes. "Have I not taught you anything? I know this because"—she pauses as she leans in closer—"I know where Little Harpe is."

"Well, ain't that some. Just so you know, there's always a treasure map, Annie." Da smiles, but it's one of them hiding smiles again. Something's astir, something as big as the storm outside. What's he keeping secret?

I look to Da, then to Annie, and back to Da. "We going treasure hunting, Da?"

"Girl, keep your voice down." He looks to me and snorts. Then he turns to Annie. "Heard tell, he was spending his last days in some Spanish jail down in Florida."

Annie shakes her finger at Da, all a-smile. "One of my boyos seen him in the Big Bayou a month back. The old river rat was bragging about his exploits to some pretty young thing. Crow knows better than to act by himself, so he comes and tells me.

By the time we git back there, that old coot is gone. But he can't have gone far. And this gets me to thinking."

Now Da wags his head. "And you bring this news to me because—"

"Because I have a plan. It's a grand plan, Tenderfoot. You remember that old talk of ours? Well, we'll have the means to do it up right." She chuckles soft, and Da nods. There's that hiding smile again. But now the two of them are wearing it. What does she mean by old talk? I'm thinking these two carry more secrets than I have the stomach to learn.

I look around the room, wondering if anyone else hears Da and Annie cooing at each other like doves. But the others are all asleep, the noise rivaling the thunder.

All of a sudden another booming crackle of thunder rolls above us. Any thoughts about the treasure are swallowed as the chickens wake up, clucking in fearsome agitation. Looking up, I hold my breath; I ain't ever seen such a thing. Wings fluttering, chickens trembling together, then jumping across the rafters. Some are flying through the loopholes.

"Da," I whisper. Something's astir.

Just then a chicken takes wing. It's cackling, near crazed in fear, and flies straight into the timbered roof. Chickens being chickens, soon the others take wing, and the flock bursts into panic.

"Da!" I bolt up. It's here. This something terrible, it found us hiding on this island.

And suddenly the fear of it sends me shivery. I feel it, what the chickens feel. The ground is atremble.

And then, that very moment, the earth explodes beneath my feet.

Chapter Four

⚓

"Da!" I'm sent flying near across the room, landing so hard I swallow my air in a single gulp. Da reaches me, takes my shoulder, and pulls me quick to my feet.

I look over the room. River pirates roll in terror, instantly awake. Some draw their pistols and fire. Others shout, spit, and wail wildly as them chickens. Annie's boyos on the benches above roll off and dangle over the fire pit. They scramble to get their footing while their brothers help pull them up to safety.

Gurdy howls in anger, looking to Da, looking to me. But instantly he's swallowed by a heap of rushing bodies. Annie disappears in the rush.

And then the thunder claps so loud, the timbers shake. Soot gathered through the ages rains down on us. Filthy nests and bird litter come a-tumbling, too. Chickens jump and fall like feathered rocks.

One man stumbles in the panic and falls into the fire pit. His screams rip the air. I hide my face in Da's sleeve, but I can't hide from the choking smells of burning flesh and feathers.

Another thunderclap, and the beams shudder. But it's not the sky rolling in thunder I discover in all fright, it's the very ground! Tables and benches are tossed upside down. Bowls, tankards, pots, anything unhinged, all tumble to the floor. Including me and Da.

"Da!" I shrill, myself a-tumbling. I tighten the strap on the case, making sure it's tight against my back. Da would whomp me good if I lost his spyglass.

"Keep your britches tied, River!" Da grabs my cuff, himself skating across the floor.

The plank floor rolls like a gathering wave. The walls, thick enough to stop bullets, begin to buckle.

The earth! The earth is tearing itself apart!

Men are shouting now, and some are screaming. We're all scrambling to stay afloat, all running to the door. But the doorway is log-jammed with bodies. No one can get through.

"Tenderfoot!" Annie booms above the mayhem. She's on the second floor with her sons. And her sons are taking an ax to a loophole.

Da swerves hard, his grip on me iron tight. I lose my feet beneath me in the force of the turnabout. He shakes me still.

From above, Annie points to the hearth. There, bodies are burning, logs are tumbling, ash and sparks spewing across the floor. As sparks meet with crumbled rushlights the animal fat crackles and bursts alive. Snakes of flame crawl across the rolling floor, eating everything—and everyone—in their reach.

Soon them flames take on a life of their own. Fed by the oil of the rushlights, the fire rages forward. It drinks in the tar and oil used in them logs. And suddenly the bunker's walls burst into flame.

I feel almighty afeared as I turn around again to see the buckling floor swallow a man whole. I can't breathe.

Da again squeezes my shoulder hard. He swings me toward the wall. I hear Annie boom more orders, but I can't quite make out the words. The smoke is swirling thick as fog now. Da battles the crushing stampede of men, himself swinging blows as hard as oak, pushing his way free from the jam.

Da drags me up the stairs. It's hard going as most of them men who didn't fall are running down. Da pushes them aside, making his way up, his fingers like talons in my shoulder. As the floor sways, the stairs sway. Some of the planks have already dropped below, feeding the fire.

Atop the stairs Da pushes me to the first loophole. This slit of a window is barely wide enough for a pollywog to wiggle through.

Suddenly I wail, knowing that's Da's plan—to push me through the window.

I scream, kicking at the wall, and swinging my fists around. "I ain't going! Not without you, Da. There's a way. Where's Gurdy?"

"You listen but good now, River. Keep that spyglass safe. You find Harpe, like Annie said. Use that glass, and it'll take you there. You remember that, *it'll take you there!* Now get to the woods, girl," he shouts, lifting me level to the window. I try to squirm out of his hold. He shakes me hard, as if to bring me to my senses. "Get to the woods, River. I promised your ma to take care of you always. And I swear, by hook, I'm a man of my word. Get on with you! Get!"

Da pushes me through the loophole. Screaming ever louder, I fall to the ground below. I land with a thud, pain burning through me like hellfire, but the wet ground softens my fall. I roll and scramble to my feet.

"I ain't leaving you!" I scream, angrier than all the thunder booming above and below. "Pull the planks away from the window! You can jump!"

"I'm right behind you, River," Da roars. "I'm right behind you always."

"There's a way!" I scream so loud, I feel my lungs rip out. "Da!"

Just then the earth convulses like a dying deer. I lose my grip and fall backward.

And the earth explodes again.

As I roll to my feet I shriek at the calamity afore me: the blockhouse is now full on fire.

"Da!" I fight the flames, beating them with all the fury I can manage. Even when my sleeve catches on fire, I beat at the flames. I know it's beating the wind now, but still I fight.

The fire gets so hot, I have to back away.

I ain't ever backed down from a fight before. And the thought of it fills me with such a fearsome rage, I can't move.

As the earth continues to rumble, the blockhouse collapses,

and the fire swallows it whole, like a starving man eating his first meal.

Get to the woods!

I stumble backward, catch myself, and stumble again. Then I run.

Chapter Five

As I'm racing to the trees I see others managed to escape the blockhouse, grown men screaming and crying. I think I see the fiddle player, but his face is near burnt off, so I'm not quite sure.

The earth convulses again, this time harder, stronger, moving like waves on a raging river. I hear grinding, like the world is tearing itself apart. The air smells of sulfur, the devil's stamp!

What's left of the blockhouse explodes.

"Da!" I stop and scream, choking on smoke and my own tears. I'm burning on the inside. And I heave, even as the earth beneath me heaves, as I fall on my hands and knees.

And then I am stunned quiet. I stare at the muddy ground. It's damp, downright wet. I ain't just kneeling in a puddle pooled from the rain; it's getting deep. The water, it's rising!

I look ahead to the woods. Suddenly, I see the big river herself rushing through the trees. Birds are screeching in panic, darting in every direction as if they lost their senses. Pine and oak, trunks as thick as barrels, sway and bow, then snap like twigs.

"Da!" I choke, my lungs burning. I know the earth done swallowed him. The earth done swallowed everyone! But who else do I call?

So I keep running because I don't know what else to do. I don't know where to go except to the river. Except to the *Molly Dear*. Home. So I call out again because that's what I always did. And he always came. "Da!"

But this time Da ain't coming.

Just then a large hand reaches out of the shadow. It seems verily the hand of God gripping my shoulder.

"Stay with me, little Tenderfoot," a familiar voice booms. Annie Christmas.

I can't see, can't catch a good swallow of air. Brush and limbs slice at my cheek and my neck. I'm running but can't feel my legs.

The sky is aglow with the fire from the blockhouse. As the flames try to jump to the trees the rain beats them down. But it ain't a blessing—the rain beats down my anger, too. And I realize I have to keep running.

Shadows blur through the woods. Water keeps rising, reaching my middle, as the earth keeps rumbling, tearing itself apart. Trees old as time are falling all around. Someone screams, and I swerve to see a tree fall on a luckless barrel of a man. He can't move, except one arm flailing wildly to his screams. I blink, and the water takes him, too.

There's another explosion, and I see a glow on the river. One of the boats has exploded, but I can't tell which one! Another boat is keel up, split in half, a fire skimming across its oily surface.

I can't see the *Molly Dear*. I want to shout, to roar in angry horror, but the sound gets lost in a gasp. The river is all aroar, a savage fury. The earth pitches again, and the river rises up . . . and swallows me whole.

Chapter Six

I dream of a copper snake. It's a large snake, and the more it coils, the larger it gets and the angrier it hisses. I dream of death coming, the Reaper's march. It strikes the palms of my hands . . .

The earth thrashes me awake, and I realize I'm on a boat.

But it ain't the *Molly Dear.*

My lungs feel like they have been ripped out. Even my voice hurts. The air is still thick with sulfur. It makes me heave up a river of innards.

"Swallowed a bit too much of the Mississip, I'd say," says Annie Christmas. "There's more fight a-coming."

"Da?" I wheeze. Next to me I find the case with Da's spyglass. I was afeared I lost it. "Da?"

"I'm sorry, child. No one seen him. But if he got out, he'll hunt you down. There's time aplenty for tears later, River. Right now, we got to move." Annie's voice roughens with urgency as she hauls me to my feet. "You got to fight it now. Let's move!"

The lightning and the fire lift the cobwebs, and I get to my feet, clinging to the case. I can see the calamity around us. Mangled wreckage floats on the water. Flatboats are pulled apart, their logs bobbing every which way. Keelboats are bottomed up, others on their side, split in half. Ropes are all a-tangle with floating chests, barrels, and timbers. A small flatboat is caught in one of them deadlier tangles. Caught in that tangle, too, is the captain of the flatter, his grisly death stare giving me the shivers.

I should be afeared, all this coming at me. But I'm stone-cold inside, watching as the big river turns on me and mine. Something else, something fierce, is brewing in the bottom of my pit. I don't see the *Molly Dear*. I don't see the *Lady Twilight* or the *Little Fanny*.

She's taken them all. That big river, she's taken away everything.

"Hold to it, boyos!" someone booms. I turn around. Cam's at the steering oar, fighting the current. There's Crow, Cay, and Cane at the poles pushing the boat into deeper waters as their brothers stand waist-deep heaving the boat away. And there's Cully standing atop the cabin shouting, "Heave, boyos!"

They're fighting to get free of the deadly tangle that's trapped us here. Dead cows, pigs, chickens, and all manner of livestock, and—I take in such a deep breath as to choke from it—all manner of humanity have become entangled in the flow.

I can hear someone screaming.

I look to see a flatboat on fire. A man's trapped inside, his bloodied arm reaching out the window of the crumbling cabin. He's pointing to the river where a black log is bobbing in the river's foam. But suddenly I see parts of it moving, and the log seems to come alive. A head turns, a head so bloody and muddy it barely seems human. And from that mask of blood and river mud, eyes the color of a sorrowful sky peer straight at me.

I jump to so fast, Annie swirls on her heels to see what's going on. I grab the cargo hook. I aim to pull that body aboard, but just then the log swirls in the wake of the dying boat and disappears beneath the foam. The man screams. But the log rights itself, the body scrambles to hold on. Then I see clinging to this body is another, smaller one, and the pip shrills like an eagle.

"Annie!" I shout, but she has already seen the struggle. Her boyos have sprung into action. Two sons scramble, hanging over the deck, using a pole to move the person toward them. Four others heave at the oars to maneuver the keel.

Annie reaches low over the side, grabs hold of the outstretched bloody arm, and pulls the two on board. The baby still screeches. The mother swoons. I take her arm, hold her upright, rushing her to the mast. I can't put her atop the cabin or she'll topple over. If I put her inside the cabin and the cabin collapses . . . so instead, I lash her to the mast, wrapping the rope tight about her. Ain't no bloodthirsty river going to take her off this boat.

"You hang on tight to that pip of yours." I secure the knot. "It's still a raggedy ride."

"Stay with me," she pleads, grabbing my arm.

"No," I take my arm back and leave her to her tears. "I got to help Annie." I'm as mad as that old river, twisting and churning, just what she done to me. I ain't got time for tears. I stand on the prow. Whatever comes my way, I mean to charge it head-on, like a bull.

Like Da.

I wave to the man across the currents. Knowing his end is nigh, he waves at us, relieved we saved his family, as he sinks into the river.

Did Da smile like that when he pushed me out the window? I turn away. That big river ain't done with us yet.

Chapter Seven

⚓

"Move, my bully boys!" Annie crows, herself rushing to the steering oar, standing at the tiller. "To oars!"

The Mississip is in a temper, a rattler with its tail twisted in a knot. That burly Cam joins his ma and throws his weight on the steering oar. On the port side are Cay and Cane, joined by another pair of twins. On the starboard side Crow and Cully and three others man oars. The brothers race to the forward and back sweeps.

Now I see the river's full rage. The water is moving in every direction, currents crashing into each other with the force of a hurricane, all aswirl in dangerous eddies. I back off the prow, easing next to Cully on the first oar.

"Hang on," he whispers tightly.

The boat twists, and I breathe a cry. I hear it, the terrible mighty roar as the big river folds in on itself, forming a double curl.

"Hell and damnation!" I scream.

There's no rowing out of the way of the monster wave; there's no steering. We're not but a twig loose on the angry, confused river. The woman tied to the mast shrieks now, burying her head in the wrappings of her pip. Even the baby is screeching in terror.

We're all hanging on, just barely.

"Courage, boys! Courage, River!" Annie roars.

The river gathers itself, twisting and turning. There's a ragged line of white snaking through the water and spray so wild, it pours like rain. The keeler rears and pitches, her wood groaning with the strain.

I point to the surface, where the water boils and bubbles.

"Brothers, brace yourself!" Cully shouts. And a plume of almighty river belches upward. Spray sweeps over the deck, near blinding me.

Suddenly, we're spinning on the edge of a giant eddy; the river is pulling us into a bottomless pit, right to hell itself. The boyos fight to keep us from falling into the watery abyss.

"Heave!" one calls out. "Heave!" the others join in.

And I shriek, "The river! She's running backward!"

The giant wave comes at us with such ferocity, I shut my eyes, knowing we're chewed up. The first crash broadsides the keeler, flying it about, just as another carries away one skiff and anything else not tied down. My own grip begins to slip until Cully seizes my hand.

Annie grabs hold of the rudder and hangs on for dear life as the wave takes us aloft.

"Who-op! This is a bit raggedy ride!" Annie shouts. "Ain't nothing we can't handle!"

From bow to stern, *Big River's Daughter* shivers in the beating.

But she holds true.

Chapter Eight

Red sky at morning, sailors take warning.

It seems forever before the river rights herself and the keeler finds her feet again. Now we drift. I'm all a-wobble, like there's no keel to keep me afloat.

All night the earth trembled.

All night the Mississip roared, angry at all creation, the smell of death thick as the devil's breath.

All night I heard people screaming, and it hurts to breathe. My heart so hurts that I look to rip it out myself.

Da . . . Where's my da? Gurdy, my keelers—all my kin, all I ever knowed in this world. That big bloodythirsty river done taken everything.

Such a big sorrow fills the back of my throat. But I swallow it anyway, even though it hurts going down, and there I drown it in this fierce rage all over again. I ain't got time for tears. I tighten the sash on the spy case, keeping it close. I look to the woman asleep with her pip, still tied to the mast. I don't even know her name, and I don't want to.

"That's my girl." I look up to see Annie at the large steering oar at the stern, her long fingers caressing the boat's wood. Her smile soft, and full of pride and relief. *"Big River's Daughter,* ain't she some piece of shiny. She got us through the night, she did."

Her smile turns even softer. "You did your da proud, little River. We'll get through this, you wait." Annie stands tall now, pulling herself up even taller. Then she calls out, "Steady, boys. Let's get her to dry land."

I grab hold of an oar as Cully and Cam take to theirs. Not every keelboat is fitted for oars—only those strong ones with a crew to match, the strongest men to work the Mississip, who could work oar and pole. Da and the *Molly Dear* had oars. And *Big River's Daughter*.

Cully's eye is bleeding, and Cam has a gash across his shoulder. Crow moans, his arm crooked where the bone snapped, and he moves to the cabin, next to the woman. But the others—Coffee, twins Cody and Coby, twins Cay and Cane, and Chance—are steady on their feet and jump to the sweeps, taking their poles. As we row, them boyos keep poles ready should anything come close and threaten the boat.

The *Big River's Daughter* follows the current downriver, moving slow and careful with the flow.

When the river becomes glassy, I jump atop the cabin to take the watch. I bring out Da's spyglass from its case. It's the last bit of him I have, so I hold it tight. I look through it to see what's ahead and what's behind.

But this river's all a-changed: whole islands gone, and a new shoreline hollowed out. The river seems as wide as the sea in places, and higher, deeper. Towns near the shore, they're gone, too.

The sky is filled with squawking gulls and ducks and herons, with cawing crows and crying geese. All swoop in confused circles, afraid to land, afraid to fly.

A canoe drifts near the keelboat. "Starboard!" I shout, and point. Inside, a dead man rolls with every pitch, eyes staring into forever, a terrible toothy grin fixed on a battered face.

He ain't alone. Others bob around us in the foamy water.

"This river, most days she's plain mean," Cully says, thumping his oar even as he wipes the blood from his eye. "Mean as all get out. But this here . . . there ain't no words for this." He shakes his head, scratches his chin.

"Port!" I point as a house floats by, riding on the current. And Cay and Cane jump to, ready to push the *Big River's Daughter* free of any dangerous tangle. Even Crow, his arm tied stiff against his body, mans the pole with one arm.

"Round to!" Annie booms, steering the keeler round the bend. And there I see all manner of boats—keelers and flatters, canoes and skiffs, and a barge as big as all—all broken and strewn like tinder across the shore. Fire gorges on their remains. Barrels bob in the waves, full of flour, apples and molasses, butter and cheese, all the lost bounty of the sunken boats.

There's not a clear space on that shore for our boat, so the boyos keep to the poles, fighting to get to the deeper water until finally letting the current take over as the rest of us keep rowing. The *Big River's Daughter* limps on downriver a ways. My shoulders ache; we're all hurting for rest. Annie hunts for another stretch below the point, free of snags and falling banks. It ain't an easy find.

But finally she calls out, "Land ho!"

The boat rocks with the waves as we ease her close to the shore, getting ready to moor her. Chance and Coffee jump deck and tie up the boat.

Finally we're grounded, out of the river and out of the calamity. My legs still feel all a-wobble, but there's no time to rest. I untie the woman, then join the boyos as they begin salvaging some of the floating timbers for repairs.

Annie taps my shoulder. "Let's get ourselves busy ashore!"

The woman with the pip follows us. Cully and Coby, each armed and readied, follow at our heels.

The shore is slick with foam and mud. Twice I slip and nearly fall, but Annie catches me by the cuff and rights me quickly. The pip screams like a shrieking banshee. The woman looks more like a walking ghost.

The path steepens to a rocky climb. Heavy black smoke roils as angry as the river across the rocks, down and across the shore. The air is thick with coal fire and furnace.

And then I rock to a halt. As ravaged as the river has been, here it is verily the end of days. Vapors thick with the devil's smell rise out of the earth in great plumes, so high and dark they hide the sun.

We've reached a small town, a mere dozen buildings. Every

which way chimneys have toppled over, setting them houses on fire. Most houses are a-crumble, nothing more than sticks. And the fire's still fierce, swallowing their remains.

"Come along now." Annie leads us, and we move forward. The woman hushes her pip.

The town is dying, struggling in its final moments. The mercantile is a heap of splinters. And in front of it is a wagon. Caught in the rumble, a tangle of oxen lie in their yokes. Clouds of flies feast on their carcasses. Chickens and geese run in circles, clucking in confusion. Running down the middle of the town comes a cow, mooing in terror, eyes rolling up to the whites.

We follow the main street around a bend, and there a small boodle of people huddle in front of the last building standing. It, too, is on fire. There's a sign of a four-leaf clover hanging on one hinge from a beam. The Lucky Inn.

Some try to fight the flames, but it's like spitting in the wind. And I rub my sleeve, trying to wipe away the memory of the blockhouse burning. A new anger is rising up in me.

Some are just standing there, lost as fallen angels. One is on her knees, head rising in prayer. Others are shouting in anger and alarm and terror.

"Why are you here?" The woman from the river, babe in arms, rushes to them. "You should run. Run!"

The kneeling woman raises her head, her eyes falling on the babe. She sobs in terror, pointing to a man fighting the flames with such tearful ferocity. I see his leg bleeding a river of blood, one hand near charred from the battle.

"My baby!" The woman screeches, pointing to the inferno. "He's still inside!"

"Cully, get back to shore. Tell them boys to start bringing the barrels up this way," says Annie. Then she rushes past the man fighting the fire.

Annie crows as she jumps through the front window, so fast and hard I hardly have time to swerve about.

"Annie!" I screech as loud as the pip. My legs wobble where I stand until I can't stand no more. The woman from the river kneels next to the other. They grip each other like long-lost sisters. All three of us watch the flames.

I hear Annie crowing on the inside and know she's found the wee pip. But I can't watch no more. Can't watch another fire, can't run away, can't move. I hide my eyes. So I can't tell how she comes through the smoke, how she breaks through the wall, and the fire, and I don't see how the man helps pull her through.

"River," I hear her coo. As I look up, I see Annie standing there. She points to the woman now holding her child. The tot is blackened from soot and smoke, but he's screaming mad. The other pip, too, joins in the wailing. Hands on her hips, Annie smiles down at me. "Ain't your da told you? There ain't no beating Annie Christmas. What you doing down there on the ground?"

"I'm not sure," I say. She eases to one knee.

She gives my shoulder a shake, whispering, "Your da and me, we were close as kin. That makes you kin. Me and the boyos, we're a motley lot, more crazy than sense. But here we are. I know you're hurting. I know it's not an easy hurt to carry. But you'll find your way when it's time. You hear me, River?"

Annie's wrong. I ain't hurting. It's more fierce, more deep, and if it could roar, it'd drown out the thunder.

"I hear you, Annie." I nod. But Da was wrong to believe in that big river. I ain't going to make the same mistake. Damn Mississip, she destroyed us all.

Chapter Nine

Civilized folk say river pirates are the scandal of human nature, the very scourge of society. Da had his own thoughts on the matter. Said Da, some had no choice, life being so hard that an honest living couldn't be had. My da, he robbed them that deserved it. He helped them who needed help, too. No one got hurt unless he had it coming. I hold to that thinking. Well, most days.

Still, civilized folk see us all the same. To them we ain't nothing but river rats. Townsfolk fear us, hunt us, and when they can, hang us. Sometimes they trade with us, if they see a profit to it.

But on this day of judgment, it's us river rats who save them.

Annie's sons set camp on the rise behind the town, not too near the edge of the woods, far from the reach of falling trees and the angry river. And to this place her sons carry up the barrels. Annie dishes out the bounty, even as townsfolk roast the chickens. We sit, peaceable enough, pirate and townsfolk eating at the same table.

The two women sit together, babes in arms. And the woman from the river no longer looks like a ghost.

The apple of sorrow ain't too big to swallow now. But ain't it true, I'm glad to be on high ground.

"Who-op!" Annie crows. It's what river rats do when they feel good about the moment. They yodel, they sing out loud.

Sometimes they fight. Sometimes they boast about fighting. But they always who-op.

"Who's this, you say?" Annie's voice bounces off the sky. "Why, it's me, Annie Christmas, just so you know! You'll be telling this story to your children, and to your children's children, so I'll make it a good one! I can outfight and outscream any critter in creation. And these fine specimens of humanity are my sons.

"This here's my eldest, Crow, once growed so eternally tall that his head was near out of sight, but then he got into a rough-and-tumble with a thunderstorm and that stunted his growth. And here be my twin suns Cody and Coby, who have the biggest feet and the widest mouths on the river, and when they grin, they are splendiferous indeed!

"Standing on one side of me, this here is Cam, who can scare a flock of wolves to total terrification, if he's a mind to, but darn if he doesn't do the biggest heap of good.

"Standing on the other side, this here is Coffee, my angel without feathers.

"Here stand my twin moons Cay and Cane, who always manage to put the two ends of everything together and help us all get along in this world.

"Here stands my Chance, just like his brother, the very sugar-maple jelly of creation.

"The youngest, Cully, takes after me, his soul full of lightning and his fist a thunderbolt, a perfect infant prodigy. So don't you worry none! We're the rough-and-tumble, can't hold us down, can't hold us back! Do your best, Mrs. Sippi, we are here to stay! Who-op!"

"Who-op!" Cam, Crow, and Cully join in, their blended voices deep as the thunder. "Who-op!" Chance and Coffee join in perfect harmony. And now Cay and Cane, and Coby and Cody, like suns and moons, dance round each other.

Them civilized folk, they clap and they laugh, and for a tick in time, they forget their woes. And then when they can't take another bite, the townsfolk sleep—under the watchful eye of Annie Christmas and her sons.

I sleep, but it's fitful, full of dreams of copperhead snakes and coiling rivers and drowning men waving good-bye. I dream of the blockhouse and hear Da shouting, *I'm behind you always!* It shivers my own timbers.

I wake in a start, full of sweat like the river done drowned me. So I sit watching the stars and hoping for morning.

It takes its time, but morning comes. Annie sends most of the boyos back to the river to drag floating timbers for the *Big River's Daughter*. The townsfolk eat hearty and swap howdies. They tell stories, and even I can see they search for hope. In short order Annie sends Cully and me to town to see what else might be found from the ruins.

"Your da was sure some," says Cully. "From the first day he showed us his true grit. Them were shinin' times."

I nod, it not occurring to me that I might be crying until he touches my cheek. It's like a wasp's sting, both the tears and the touch. I swat at them both.

Cully chuckles until I shoot him a prickly look.

"I never knew my own pa." Cully nods. "But I know if I lost my mam, my heart would surely break so."

"You didn't know your da?"

"None of us knew our fathers." Cully smiles.

Then I see it, how twins Cay and Cane are light tan and blue eyes, while Coffee and Crow are as deep a black as crows' feathers, with eyes just as dark. And Cully himself, eyes green as spring corn, is a-shining tea ebony. Them are the boys of Annie Christmas, and no other—no man or otherwise—lays claim to them.

Cully laughs. "Can't tame Annie Christmas, any more than you can tame that big river. They're one and the same, Mam and the Mississip."

I smile, if only slight. A pirate ain't one to follow rules of civilized folk. Maybe that's why them folks fear and hate us. I wonder, looking over my shoulder at them townsfolk safe in the morning sun, would they remember it were Annie and her sons, river rats and colored—a deadly pairing for some—that saves them, watches over them, keeps them safe?

I shake my head. I expect they won't. Da always said, easier to float a boat up some grizzled falls than to change a righteous man's wrong thinking.

I say, "I ain't ever knew my ma. Da had real heart feelings for her. Said he, he believed in three things. Ma. That big river. And me. But looky here: ain't none of us done right by him. Ma died when I was born. The river killed him. And—and I ran away. . . ."

"For certain, grief can change the way we see things, River. But the river ain't killed your da any more than you killed your ma. Your da don't blame you. And you did what you had to do back there on the island. Just like him."

But I don't swallow his jagged thinking. "Da said, the river will always do right by us. But look where she took us. Look what happened to all them keelers. Look what happened to that town. That river, she ain't done right to no one."

"You think believing in something is easy, only for those times when life goes easy? Girl, believing in something when it's near impossible to do so, that's called faith. Your da, he had faith in you. And don't tell me you ain't put your da through some trying times. He didn't give up on you. Maybe the river didn't give up on you, either."

"You a preacher now?" I growl, crossing my arms. Anger's churning in me easy enough, leaving a sour taste behind, and I spit.

"Not me. I aim to misbehave most times. But still, maybe it weren't no luck that Ma pulled you out of the river. Maybe it was the river bringing you to her."

We reach the edge of town. In that very moment the earth rolls again. At first, I expect it to go away, just like the other trembles. But the roll deepens, the grinding gets louder.

Suddenly, I trip, stumbling to the ground. For a long

moment I lie still, squeezing out my breath. My heart is pounding like a stampeding horse afeared of its own shadow. I look up to the field. The earth is buckling like a washboard. Fountains of vapor erupt down the line, all the way to the woods.

"Hell's bells!" I shout to Cully. "The ground is tearing itself up again!"

Two full strides ahead, Cully shouts, "Ain't no time to take a nap, girl! We got to get out of here!" He points to the other side of town, to the river, to his brothers. It's our only way out.

I roll to my feet and run, jumping the bricks of the tumbled chimneys, weaving past the burnt remains of the ramshackled buildings.

A tear in the earth rips down the middle of the main street. With every tremble the chasm widens. We veer sharp to sounds of ripping wood. I glance back just in time to see the Lucky Inn tumbling into the abyss.

As the earth opens, it spews sand and water and black vapor in a hot fountain. Even the flies feasting on the ox carcasses roll over dead. The oxen and wagon teeter on the edge of the crevice, then fall into the vapor and explode into flame.

Cully runs and jumps, gathering speed. It's all I can do to keep up; I'm too afeared not to. By the time we reach the bluff overlooking the river, the earth behind us is shredded, the remains of the town wrapped in a black fog.

The earth bellows now.

I fly down the slope. Cully seizes me by the shoulder and pulls me along like a raggedy doll.

"Heave to! Heave to!" He waves to his brothers, who are already cutting the keel free, heaving into the poles, pushing the keeler away from the shore.

Just then my legs fail me, like they're not even mine. I can't go back on that bloodythirsty river. I stand there watching the water roiling in anger, just like before, knowing it'll swallow us whole.

"River!" Cully shouts. "Move it! Get to the boat!" But he doesn't wait for an answer. He runs back to me and swoops me over his shoulder. My ears burn at the roar of rushing waters. I squeeze my eyes shut as he jumps aboard.

In the distance the town explodes on itself. Cam takes command at the steering oar while his brothers now man oars, moving the big keeler into the current, away from shore. Together, they heave with the strength of a team of oxen. I jump atop the cabin, just like I always do. But I can't watch. This big river, she ain't ever going to stop until she swallows us all.

"Port!" Cully points to a tangle of rope, driftwood, and other snags snaking near portside. Annie's sons, all them strings on a fiddle, move in harmony. They heave the keel forward, weaving through the tangle and squeezing through the ripples. Foam washes over the deck.

Another explosion rocks the shore. All our heads swerve about, to see the bluff tear itself apart in a geyser of sand, foam, and water, and tumble down. The river roils anew, pitching the keeler hard.

"Heave, brothers!" Cam shouts.

Them boyos push harder. Coby pushes so hard, his nose begins to bleed.

I turn away from the river, watching Cam take us around a curve. And for a moment, on the lee side of the bend, the water becomes almost serene, as if nothing happened at all.

The keel once again limps close to shore, and Annie's boyos now scramble to secure her. I think of Annie and search the shoreline. There's no trace of her or the townsfolk.

Well, I ain't waiting. I aim to get off this river now.

I run across the deck and fly off the bow. I don't stop running as I hit the water, then I race through the woods, weaving through the tangle and bush. This time I know I'm crying. I'm roiling mad, but I use the anger to make me go faster.

I'm right behind you always!

Da pushed me through the window because he knew I don't give up. And he knew that I could go on without him if I had to.

Damn that river! She hates us all! And I hate her right back!

I turn about, and finally I see Annie Christmas. She's

rounding up what's left of them townsfolk. They look as ragged and torn as I feel, dragging themselves along behind her. Annie turns, them pearls sparking in the light. She smiles as she sees me, and waves me on.

I got my feet under me now. I'm running straight up to her, that giant of a woman, and wrapping my arms around her as far as I can reach. And for a moment I stand there, hanging on for dear life.

Part Two

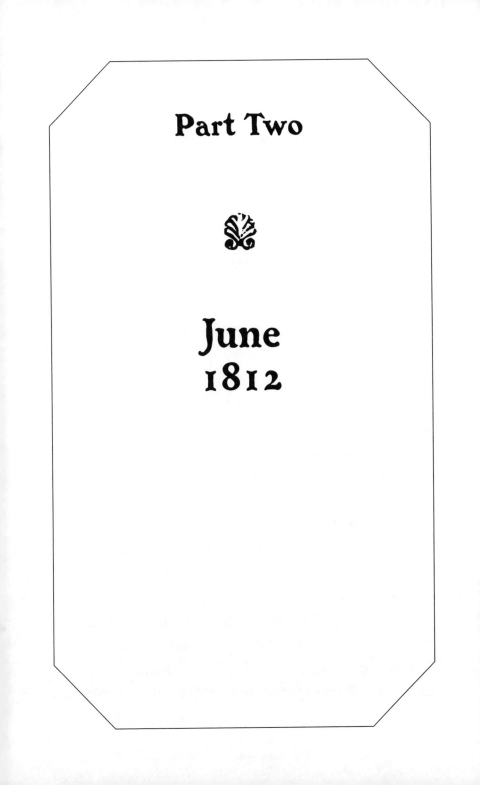

June
1812

For four months the earth shakes, and two shakes tremble as big as the day the river ran backward. I was afeared all right, downright shivery even in the heat-heavy air. It ain't so bad in the day, because I can see what's ahead and what's behind. But I hate the night, especially that tick in time just after the sun sets. That's when the big birds fly back to their roosts and sing them noisy songs. Then when them big birds quiet, the night birds begin their whirring.

Before the quakes I looked forward to them noises. Da called it river song. He and I would listen to it, him smoking his corn pipe. Said Da, the river ain't really ever quiet. Unless a storm comes.

After the quake the river night got quiet. And I shiver, hoping it didn't mean another storm was brewing, another wave coming.

I'm always dog alert for the next storm.

I'm right behind you always.

The Big River's Daughter stays moored as near to the crumbled town as we dare. It's slow going, fixing up the keeler. Says Annie, "Love her like one of your own. It's what keeps her afloat. Take good care of her, and she'll do right by you. It's what makes her home."

Them townsfolk slowly find their legs. I hear them talk about the homes they lost and about the kin they lost. I feel as chewed up as them. Seems like in times afoul, we ruffians and them civilized folk are more alike than not.

Meanwhile, I keep busy cleaning the deck, retwining the

rope, and knotting a net. I help Cully repair the cabin, plank by plank. I help Coffee and Chance fit new oars, and I help Cay and Cane prepare the deck timbers as Coby and Cody repair the deck. I take care of the Big River's Daughter, and in that caring I feel my spirit calm.

Then one day the woman we pulled from the river asks me if I'd like to go with her when she gets ready to move out with the rest of them civilized folk. Seems the life of a keeler is no place for a proper young lady.

But there's nothing proper about a daughter of a river rat, so she leaves without me.

Eventually, the Big River's Daughter is afloat, even if she ain't her shiny self. We make our way downriver to New Orleans. No one's trading, because there's nothing to trade. No one's needing transport, because there's no place to go and no money to pay for it. And Annie Christmas, like my da, believes it a special sin to take from them who have nothing left for themselves. Seems like every minute of the day, the Reaper stands just off our prow waiting for our last breath.

In June 1812 the eighteen states united declare war on the British Empire for the second time. Them British are still mightily riled over losing the first time. But then they got into another bloody rough-and-tumble with France. Hoping to stay out of the affray, Jefferson called an embargo in 1807, stopping all trade with them and most other foreign countries. But the law hurt American traders, and three days afore he left office in 1809, Jefferson took back his law. The damage was done, however, and the new president found himself in the middle of a mad hornet's nest. There's been too many—Spanish, French, and even uppity Americans—telling us what to do and how to do it, too many telling us where to live and how to live. That's why Da began his life on the Mississip.

Ain't no one going to tell me how to live my life but me.

I just don't know where I belong anymore. I'm all afloat, like them loose timbers on the current.

Chapter Ten

⚓

And then I see them spires of New Orleans rise on the horizon. Every keeler, every flatter, everyone who works the river knows New Orleans. It's where the money flows in the world of river and sea trade.

There's river wild, and then there's city wild. And New Orleans is the wildest of the wild, Da said. It ain't a city for the weak-bellied. More snakes than grass creep in the city's hidey-holes. More rats fill the streets than hairs on a dog's back. Most summer days the heat melts your skin right off, and worse than the heat are the armies of skeeters.

It's an odd city built on a cleared swamp. The river bends around it, with natural levees on one side and a ribbon of high ground that slopes gentlelike off the river. Then the earth falls away into mosquito-ridden swamp. Beyond the swamp is Lake Pontchartrain. Every storm that flies off the ocean, every time the river surges, every time the lake stirs up a froth, all that water floods into the city, and with it comes all manner of rot and vermin. All that filth flows through the streets in open ditches and streams to the swamp.

And rising from all that festering is every stink imaginable. To cover the smell, city folk plant sweet-scented trees and brush, orange and fig, azalea and camellia.

But it all mingles into one almighty stink, one I can smell as we float closer to the city.

Tall oaks old as time and tupelos draped with moss line the

edge of the riverside. Wild grapes weave through the branches of the pawpaw trees.

It seems too peaceable, the river so gentle now. I turn back to the keeler's deck. The *Big River's Daughter* is still a sorry sight. She's looking as all-overish ill as I feel, but she's staying afloat.

It's near noon as we make our way to the levee. I ain't ever seen the docks so crowded. All manner of life, including them who survived the river's wrath, are stacked three deep along the wharves. There's keelers and flatters. Moored are the low-lying red-sailed boats of the oystermen. And just beyond, schooners with their tall masts touching wispy clouds rock on the wake. Men on boat and dock shout and curse at each other, unloading barrels and crates of sugar and rice, bales of cotton and stacks of lumber. Horses, pigs, chickens, and cattle roam the docks.

There's whole families of flatters, even their women and children. They leave their boats behind, selling the wood and taking everything they own on their backs.

Such a tangle of confusion brings out thieves and river-bottom scavengers waiting to barter their goods stolen from poor folk.

Annie crows again as her boyos row up to the dock. Chance throws a rope. The man on the dock catches it, pulling it tight and securing it quickly. For a few minutes the deck is a-flurry with motion as we settle her in.

That's when I see them. Men limping, men burnt, some with arms still wrapped in bandages. It shakes me as deep and thunderous as that quake, burning like a fresh wound. The men from the blockhouse.

Maybe Da . . . I scarce put such a thought into words. It's more like a breath. My fingers tingle with the cold heat of it.

Da would look for me here. Annie said as much, didn't she?

Already I know my next move—when suddenly we are set upon by a pair of codfish dandies.

I stare for a long moment. Them are brothers, true enough, dressed in some fancified trousers, black coats over ruffled shirts. They tip their wide-brim hats, revealing black hair pulled back into fine tails, muttonchops framing their ebony, straight-jawed faces. They stand too oak-straight to have ever worked on a deck. They smile the same toothy smile, not a one rotted brown from hunger.

Ain't they the biggest toadies in the puddle. I grin, watching Annie take one of their hands with a strong grip.

"Ah, Alain! Good as always to see you!" Annie gives it a rough shake. The man clears his throat. His smile stiffens as he withdraws his hand.

Cully bends low to my ear. "Don't let them soft exteriors fool you none," he whispers. "They own a sugar plantation inherited from their mother, a free colored married to a French planter. They own one of the fastest schooners in these parts and hire themselves out to the highest bidder. They're sharp as gator's teeth, filled with venom."

"*Bonjour! Bonjour, jolie dame!*" The other man smiles real pretty.

Annie turns to him and smiles even prettier. "And you, Alaire, are looking quite the rogue."

Alaire chuckles. Waving his lacy sleeve in the air, he bows.

As I come up behind Annie their smiles sharpen when they look at me.

"And who is this *peu de perle?*" says Alain. "Another pearl for your collection?"

His look, like a viper's hiss, sets me a-scowl.

Annie's smile cools. "Careful, Alain, this little pearl bites."

"Ah," says Alain. He twists his lip as if he's chewing an onion. "She's *Américaine.*"

Annie snorts. "Now, friend, Louisiana has been part of these here United States for almost two months now. And that means we're all Americans."

"Perhaps," says Alain, raising a ruffled cuff to his nose. "But my heart remains *français.*"

Annie pushes me behind her as she moves forward. "Well, as much as I love swapping howdies with you, I'm sure you're not here by accident. Did *he* send you here? Or you looking for other favors? You hoping to get a dock fee out of me?"

"You wound us, *jolie dame!*" says Alaire. "You think us common criminals?"

Annie wags her head and chuckles. "Ah, boyos, there's nothing common about you. But all howdies aside, I need to see him."

Alain bows, his arm sweeping in front of them as if to show the way.

I get ready to jump ashore, aiming to check out the docks. But Cully stops me, bending low to my ear.

"It don't look it from here," Cully says. "All them people living on top of each other, next to each other, the French and the Spanish, the slave and the immigrant. But mark me, everyone knows their proper place."

"Ain't none of us proper, Cully. You saying I need to know my place now?" I growl.

"I'm saying, your da was well-respected in all parts of New Orleans. Even his enemies thought him some. If nothing else, they feared him mightily, and they didn't try their luck against him. But your da, he ain't here. He had enemies enough, and no doubt word's out about what happened." He holds his arm up next to mine, his with the shine of deep Indian tea, mine with the fuzz of a tanned peach. "This here city sees colored and it sees white. And there's no place in that city where both fit with any comfort. Make no doubt, despite their smiles they hate each other. For you they'll see a river rat, the pip of the king of the river pirates. Then they'll hunt you down because of past grievances with your da. Do you hear me, River? I want you to understand my full meaning here."

"Don't you worry none about me." I face him, eye to eye.

I watch Cully and Chance jump after their ma. I watch as Coffee, Cay, and Cane take to the docks in search of supplies. I watch them all as they disappear into the sea of heads. My eyes roam the dock, looking for them men from the blockhouse.

I turn to face the deck of the *Big River's Daughter*. It's just me, and burly Cam, and twins Cody and Coby.

True enough, I hear you, Cully. But you're expecting me to

stay put, and that ain't going to happen. Not if there's a chance my da is out there.

"River," Cam calls out, and I turn about. Slowly. He needs help on another panel. I stand there for a moment, already feeling sorry for what I'm about to do.

Seems Cody and Coby know what I'm about to do, too. They turn from their work on the stern. All three are watching me with an eagle's stare.

Da always complained I didn't know how to stay put.

Cam stiffens. He shakes his head slow, wagging his finger. "Don't you give it a thought, River. Mam will skin me if I don't do right by you."

It gives me pause, for Annie's done right by me. I look to the river. This here whole town, they feared my da. They feared him something powerful. If he's alive, he needs my help. I aim to find him.

"Can't no one be more heartful than me for all you done," I say, standing my ground, tall as my da. "But if I was out there and Da was here, ain't nothing could stop him from looking for me. He's my da. I'm going. . . ."

Cam scratches his chin. Cody and Coby put down their hammers, stepping forward. I'm watching all three now, and watching the dock.

Cam pulls himself up and takes one menacing step forward. He's shaking his head.

I grin back. He's a mountain of a man. He thinks by standing so tall, casting his long shadow over me, I won't dare move.

I say, "I'll be back before you can spit proper." Then I bolt to the dock, gathering speed even as I land. I don't look back, running head-on into the city wild.

Chapter Eleven

I weave through boodles of people, fighting my way toward the flatboat where I saw them damaged men from the blockhouse. But by the time I get to the mooring place, the flatters are already taking it apart. And them keelers are already gone.

I stand still for a moment, trying to get my bearings. I throw a glance backward. I can't see Cam, but I know he's coming. I expect him to tan my hide but good when he catches me.

If he catches me.

I look to the market street, and then to the city past them street callers. I shoot off like a musket ball, running through the maze of narrow streets. There's people everywhere, walking, running, working, and shouting and singing. The streets are no longer cobblestoned, but are greasy and slippery black soil. Carriages move slowly through the sludge, and sometimes not at all. Sidewalks are planks pegged into the ground. Sometimes wooden drains line the streets, but mostly it's just plain ditches.

But for all this muck, street vendors howl, holding platters of honey cakes and ginger cakes. There's slave women groups all dressed in the same raggedy linen and calico aprons, each color telling which plantation they belong to. Some wear prettified headwraps, the only thing to call their own. They sell vegetables and fruits and all manner of fish. Banana sellers walk by, balancing their yellow-and-green crop on their heads. Children race between them, begging for pralines.

There's a small gathering of slaves dressed in same-colored cotton trousers and shirts, two pounding drums with a third fifing a melody. Another plays on a four-string banjo. Women and children are dancing in circles.

There's some speaking French, and some singing Spanish. There's more, too—more languages than feathers on a bird. So much clucking, it sounds like a farmyard. It smells like one, too. Animals roam in every direction, marking their passage with heaps of dung. On every corner shops and taverns are filled with the spicy, pungent, tangy smells of cooking food. The stink from the ditches rises up to meet the smells of the market. Even the devil can't breathe this much noise and stink.

Just then I hear somewhere a fiddle's playing, and there's a banjo fighting to keep up with the melody. A raw tear rises at the sound of it, and I find myself looking for that fiddle. My fingers tremble tightening the strap on my spy case.

I'm a dozen blocks from the river. The mud seems greasier, the streets narrower. Here the buildings are made from the lumber of old flatboats and lean against each other, just a tumble away from falling down. Da warned me about this place. I'm in the Swamp: the meanest, muckiest blocks in the whole of New Orleans. It's a place of saloons and dance halls and hideouts for all the river scum. This here place is the most vicious wild in New Orleans.

On the corner I pass a boodle of corned sailors and soldiers squaring off in a street game of cards. Flatters look on, waiting for a chance at luck. The music lures me to a corner tavern where a sign hangs crooked above the door: Sure Enuf Hotel.

I walk into a dark room, thick with smells from the river, the market, the city, and the fire pit. Lanterns hang from the low ceiling. Sitting in their glow are the lowest of river-bottom scum. *Caboteurs* in their red hats gather in one corner. Keelers shout insults to flatters. Flatters shout insults to soldiers and sailors. Everyone's poking for a fight.

In the far corner of the tavern, standing in the kitchen, is one big barrel of a woman. She dances a jiggity jig to the fiddler's tune. Her corn pipe bobs to the fiddling, and with every jump the tankards bounce and the pots rattle.

They're all a-laughing, a-drinking, all too corned. Ain't no one sees a pip like me slip through the shadows. I inch across the wall, looking into each face as the fiddler stomps and plays in the center of the room. He starts up another tune. This one's fast, and sudden it stings me with the bite of a thousand wasps.

I let loose a sharp breath, and I jump from the pain of it.

Then the fiddler turns, and lantern glow lights the shadows on his face. A dark patch wraps his eye and ear and cheek. His face is scarred red, but I know him, true enough.

He's the fiddler from the blockhouse.

And then the fiddler sees me, too.

Chapter Twelve

"Thar!" the fiddler booms. He uses his bow to point me out. Hell's bells! They seen me the moment I walked in! They've been watching me! Lightning-quick, three others jump to and surround me. I swerve, ready to jump atop a table. An old sausage as gnarly as an old twisted oak blocks me.

"What we have here, my boyos, some wee river rat off the streets?" That old sausage smiles none too pretty, his teeth rotting brown. He moves closer and grins, his breath reeking. "News gets around when Annie Christmas floats in, especially when it's told that that old salt Fillian's whelp is on board. Have to say, you made this easy coming into our little home. Thought our little rat hunt would take a long while."

I step back. Don't I know now, Cully tried to warn me that Da's enemies might hunt me down, might just kill me outright, or keep me alive just long enough to learn what I know about Da's trading routes. I didn't listen.

"You let me go," I growl. "I'm a-warning you."

The old sausage bends low, facing me eye to eye. His glee is downright evil, as evil as his breath. "Ain't you the wee pip of that snapping turtle? It's me, Hogg Tyler, brother to Plug. Heard tell your pa and my brother swapped howdies on Union Island the day before the big river swallowed it up?"

He moves fast for an old sausage. His arm shoots out like a viper, seizing me by the shoulder. His fingers dig into me like a bear trap, right down to the bone. I wince hard, stumbling in pain.

"You'll forgive mister biggity here." That big barrel of a woman comes my way, too. She's grinning sideways. "Just call me Mother Colby, my dear. We just need to talk."

Hogg Tyler loosens his grip, but just enough to ease the pain. Says him, "You mind your manners, wee missy." I relax my shoulders. And he eases his hold. That sausage thinks I'm backing down.

"Your pa, he was a real hair of the bear," says Mother Colby. "He built hisself up quite the trade. He held it with an iron grip. Well, now the king is dead. It leaves the door open for all sorts of opportunity for them strong enough to take it."

I stand still enough. And that old sausage eases his hold all the more. He don't expect me to fight. And that's when I strike. I swing a leg around, first kicking him in the ankle. As he wheels about to swipe me I make another wide kick, right in the nethers. He crumbles over, choking.

I drop on the floor, moving on my back like a crab. I kick like an angry mule, shrilling like a banshee. And whenever one comes close enough to grab me, I scratch and bite and kick again.

That Mother Colby waddles my way. She reaches out, hoping to grab my leg. I kick her, too.

Others in the tavern stand, some just watching, grinning ear to ear. But more throw their heads back laughing. They hoot and holler, "Who-op!"

"Seems like Fillian's whippersnapper got your goats!" one shouts. "My money's on her!"

"You're some, Hogg Tyler. If you can't control that little whelp, how can you take over as king of the river?"

Soon enough there's more hollering and more laughing as more keelers and flatters and street ruffians join the affray. Some tumble over tables, swinging at anything that moves. Hogg Tyler raises his hand, demanding order. But the room ignores him.

"If this were my da's brigade"—I grin back at the old sausage and kick again—"not one man could ignore his hand or question his order." I ain't letting him near me, try as he might.

"Get that pip!" Mother Colby shouts. Then Hogg Tyler withdraws his pistol from his belt. He lowers it at me. He's smiling as he pulls back the hammer.

The room goes quiet. Even I go quiet. He ain't one to shoot a pip, is he? I can feel my fingers tremble, and I squeeze my hands closed, making a fist. I ain't closing my eyes. He's going to have to look me straight on if he shoots me.

But it ain't him that fires a shot. The room jumps as a shot explodes above their heads.

"Listen up!" someone booms. "Girl, listen up!"

Only then do I look away from that old sausage. I turn around to see Cam filling up the doorway.

"Now, what brings a colored son of Annie Christmas to my reputable establishment?" Mother Colby bellows.

Hogg ain't lowering his pistol just yet. He's still aiming it at my head.

"Not staying long," says Cam. He aims his second pistol at Hogg. "Just picking up what's mine. Get to your feet, girl!"

"Colored man can't shoot a white man." Mother Colby shakes her head. "You'll get yourself hung before the sun sets."

"What about shooting a lily-livered codfish?" Cam smiles back. He ain't lowering his pistol.

Everyone knows the sons of Annie Christmas. Ain't no one shooting one of them sons. The shooter risks the full wrath of Annie Christmas dogging him the rest of his life. Annie be seeking more than a pearl for that wrong.

And Annie Christmas always wins.

Hogg Tyler backs down, returning the hammer in place. He even smiles, waving his hand to get me to my feet.

But it ain't no *man* that takes on the son of Annie Christmas. In a tick of time, another shot screams through the room. I snap around. There's wisps of smoke curling about Mother Colby's head.

Mother Colby done shot Cam!

Cam swerves hard against the wall. He crumbles to the floor with a growl.

Now I scream, but not out of fear for my life. I'm shivery all right, my blood boiling mad. But burrowing deep inside, like some bloodsucking worm caught in my belly, is shame. I scream because it's me that done brought Cam here. I made a mess out of all this. And I got Cam killed.

I'm still screaming when Hogg's fingers become a vise around my neck. He squeezes me quiet.

"Let me be plain here," he says. "I've a task to do, and you're useful in that doing. But the moment you become too much a nuisance to me and my plans, I'll dispose of you as I would any trash. You hear me, whelp?"

Now for sure, I'm done for. Just like Cam. Just like Da.

I look at him and give a slow nod.

Chapter Thirteen

There's a few truths about river pirates, Da once told me. For the most part them are liars and thieves. Most pirates be half a bubble off plumb. A few almighty talk like a book, but they think like a slug. Despite living on the river, most pirates are deathly afeared of water and swim as if each leg was filled with lead.

And most river rats are surely bad shots with a pistol, even when standing an arm's-length away.

"You river-bottom bilge rat!" Cam shouts at that murderous Mother Colby. "You shot my foot!"

I'm breathing easier now that the smoke is cleared. But that worm of shame still burrows through my belly.

"At least you ain't dead." Hogg stands tall as others gather around the fallen Cam. Quickly the old sausage takes control of the room. And that weasel fiddler, smiling extra pretty, winks at me. I jump at him. Hogg Tyler tightens his hold, squeezing the air right out of me.

"Don't rightly want to kill one of them sons of Annie Christmas, but you mind yourself, boy," says Mother Colby. "Or that little whelp dies. No one will mourn the missing of a nonesuch."

Now Hogg nods his head in the direction down the hall to a door. Only then does he let loose his hold, tossing me to another. "Take them two to the shed."

"When I find my da"—I cough, wheezing to breathe—"he'll do you in but good."

"You're full of spit, all right." Hogg grins. "I admire that. Maybe once we're done, I won't kill you after all."

Hogg's man drags me down the dark passage and through the back door. From there it's a short walk to the shed. He tosses me inside like a sack of flour. A moment later, two men toss Cam. He groans as he hits the floor. It's the fiddler who locks us in. A new anger roils up in me, burning fresh and raw.

There's but a sliver of dayglow escaping a loophole near the ceiling.

"River," Cam groans. He eases his back against the wall, holding his foot, peeling away the boot. "Don't you ever stay put?"

"Must hurt some powerful." I wince. Ain't enough light to see his foot, but it smells bloody enough.

"No more than you will when Mam gets ahold of you," he growls in his pain.

"I expect so," I say. Don't I know, I deserve whatever Annie Christmas brings my way. But worrying about what's coming ain't going to get us out of this pickle. "Right now, you need some wrapping for that foot of yours. We need a way out."

Cam chuckles. "So it ain't going to help none if I say just stay put? It won't take long before Mam finds out what happened and comes looking for us."

"I expect not." I grin.

But then I hear someone clearing a throat. Both of us jump to. Cam stands a bit wobbly on one leg. But me I grab the first thing I can wrap my fingers about, a large wooden stick. Ain't much I can do, but Da taught me, you just have to give it all you got and hope for the best.

"Who's there!" I boom, sounding taller than I might.

"Answer the girl!" Cam booms, his voice the very thunder of creation.

"River?" a voice rasps. "That you, little River?"

And a grief swallows me whole again, just like it did before. I can scarce breathe.

Because that voice, I know that voice.

I move toward that sliver of light falling on a burly figure. He lies on the floor, his foot shackled to a post in the corner.

I wince, for rats had been chewing on his toes and ankles, and blood pools on the floor beneath. The man rattles his chains as he turns my way. I see him, even in the shadows. His chin whiskers are burnt almost to a nub. His halo of hair is all but gone, and he wears a patch over one eye. His hand is wrapped in a bloody red bandana. There's a bright scar across his cheek.

"You a ghost come to haunt me?" My heart beats so hard, it hurts in my chest.

"No be thinking a ghost can hurt this much," he sputters.

Right then, don't you know it, a rabbit can't jump as fast as me. I swallow the big man in a hug. Even though he winces in pain, I ain't letting go. And I cry now for all creation.

"Gurdy!"

Chapter Fourteen

Gurdy says, "I no see your da and you, so I only hope you free of them flames. It a fight to get free myself. I think I no too long in this life. My face be on fire, but the pain no as hurtful as me old heart. But I live, and I run crazy. I get free just as the blockhouse blows. And then I see Annie Christmas pull you from the river.

"But I no believing your da dead. He no dead, not Dan Fillian. He too ornery for heaven, too mean for the devil. I know if any could get free of that fire, he can."

Gurdy coughs. He carries this same heavy anger as me. I rest my hand on his shoulder. He takes it in his big hand, a glitter of a tear rolls down his scarred cheek. I sit right up close to him.

Says Gurdy, "Some flatters take me aboard, and I find my way downriver, slow but sure. Take a long while to get my legs back under me. But when I do, I go look for you. I seen a lot of wrath in my day, them revolts in Santo Domingo, the uprising on the plantation. But on the river those first days, I no ever seen so much evil and wrath. Then it a new day when I reach the city. I think, this is where she take you. Walking through the market square, I get swiped by that scallywag Hogg Tyler. Him and that fiddler. This Mother Colby carry a few plans for me." Gurdy shakes his legs, rattling his chains.

Now I cry. "Don't rightly make sense all the sorrow that brought us downriver. Hogg Tyler is one bad egg. I won't be missing him none when we leave. But true enough, here you are, and here I am. It were the doings of that rapscallion himself that brought us together. And for that, I'm downright heartful.

You get your rest. Then you wait. They'll see. It'll be the end of their days."

Cam growls, "Glad you two are having such a fine time of it. That woman shot my foot, and I aim to have a piece of her for it."

Chapter Fifteen

There ain't no way out but the way we came in—through the door. So I wait, stick in hand. Cam's waiting, too. Anyone who comes in, we aim to crack his lice but good.

All night I wait at the ready. Gurdy dozes, but it's a fitful sleep. He trembles and moans, his chains rattling with his every twitch. Cam dozes, too. He's more a-growl.

Just as a ripple of dawnlight spills through that loophole I hear someone scraping heels on the planks outside. Someone shouts, setting others scrambling. Then someone pulls the bolt back and lifts the jam.

Gripping my stick tight, I swing it as far back as I can.

Gurdy stirs awake, his chains rattling, and he raises to his feet. Cam, too. We're ready.

The door creaks open. A wash of lantern light drifts through the way. A tall shadow moves forward.

I swing with all my might. But fast as any wild river flow, this big shadow blocks my blow with his cane. He twists his cane in the air like a sword. He sends my wood stick across the room.

And I stand still, weaponless. Cam jumps forward, but his foot pains him and he can't move fast enough. The man swings his cane about, just that fast. Had it been a sword, he would have cut out Cam's heart. But as it was just a cane, he thumps Cam's chest. Cam backs down.

He's a tall man, a real highborn, in a wide-brim hat. Despite the swampy heat he's wearing a fancified waistcoat and a coat the color of dawnlight, with high, stiff boots. His fair skin shines in the light, but not so shining as them gold eyes, gold with layers of green. Side whiskers dress up his cheeks. He's taking in all our faces with a glare like an eagle's eye.

Just then he grabs my chin. I wince in his almighty strong grip.

"Do you know who I am, girl?"

I nod. "You being the city patroon." Like my da was king of the river, this here highborn is king of the city. He's the one that calls all the shots.

Now the man relaxes and lets me go with a smile. "True enough."

He taps his cane against the floor, and two rush into the room. One is Mother Colby herself, and she looks in a worm of worry. She scuttles to Gurdy to unlock his shackles, then turns, looking to the patroon. She's sweating some. I see it, how she fears this man. It's the same look river folk gave my da. She ain't liking this unexpected visit.

Mother Colby gives me an angry glance. Crossing my arms and standing tall as I might, I say, "I warned you."

The patroon cocks his head, and Mother Colby scuttles quick out the shed.

The man standing with the patroon is a surgeon dressed in fine white linen and a straw hat. Easing next to Cam's foot, he peels away more of the boot and wipes away blood.

"This isn't good," he says to the patroon. "But it's not as bad as it could be. Boy, this is going to hurt some. I'll try to make it quick."

The surgeon hands Cam a bottle of rum. From the smell of it, it's fresh off the boat. Cam looks to the patroon.

"Drink it, boy," says the patroon. "It'll take the edge off." The patroon himself takes hold of Cam's shoulder while he takes a swig.

"Will I dance fine?" says Cam, bracing himself. "The ladies like the way I dance."

"Stay strong, boy," says Gurdy.

"You have plenty of dances left," says the surgeon, pouring the rum on a knife. Then without stopping the rum flow, he pours it on the bloody wound. Cam yowls like a wounded cat. The surgeon gives Cam a stick to bite down on. With a nod to the patroon, the surgeon keeps his promise, working as fast as a spider spinning a web. He cuts the toe free from the foot. He sews the flap shut. Cam clenches his teeth on the stick so hard, I think he's about to bite right through his jaw. He forces himself to breathe, hard, heavy, fast breaths through his teeth. I hold him down as best I can, gnashing my own teeth.

And then it's done. Cam swoons, out cold.

The surgeon takes a swig of what's left in the bottle. He passes it to the patroon, who takes a swig of his own.

"Put them two in the carriage outside," says the patroon to others behind him. He points to me. "But this little pip, she rides with me."

Taking my spyglass, I leave the shed. Mother Colby stands in her kitchen, smiling sideways until the patroon throws her a glance. She loses that smile.

Hogg Tyler winks at me, and I know it a warning. I ain't seen the last of him. Or of Mother Colby.

I look to the fiddler. I ain't seen the last of that snake, either.

Chapter Sixteen

"A fine warm day for a ride, don't you think?" The patroon smiles, dipping his hat to a passerby. The footman holds the door open as he steps into the carriage.

And it's a mightily grand carriage, as large as any I seen, white with a fancified crest painted on the door. Its top is down, folded half in front and half in back. It's led by a pair of some high-stepping prancers.

From his post atop a box, the driver watches me with mousy eyes and a twitchy nose. Sitting next to him is a man armed with two pistols and a musket. He stands sharp, looking for trouble from any who walk too close to the carriage. I expect his aim is just as sharp.

I look at the carriage behind us, black with no painted crest, its top folded against the back. From there Gurdy sends me a smile as another man and the surgeon help Cam aboard.

"Hurry along, *petite* River." The patroon taps two hard strikes against the floor. The driver bows his head as I climb into the carriage, and then he snaps his whip. The two prancers jump to, at the ready.

The footman shuts the carriage door. He runs out in front, and there he stays, clearing the way. On the street the sea of sailors and soldiers stop playing their cards and drinking; the keelers and flatters stand quiet. All part like waves, letting the carriages sail through. A few hail the patroon. He waves back.

The carriage rounds one corner, then a second, back down to the river. She sparkles into view as we approach the levee. I look at her for a long while, the anger rising like it had that first day. But then the anger's done, and I bow my head. Now it's just sorrow welling up in me. Looking up, I notice the patroon watching me. I wag off my sorrow and stiffen my shoulders, sitting tall as I might.

Men turn about, dipping their hats. Women in their Sunday finery flutter their fancy fans. Children chase the carriages, waving and begging. The patroon smiles.

Church bells are a-ringing across a large green. I see a boodle of men and women listening to three men playing fiddles. But some fiddles! One is as big as the man himself. I ain't ever heard such a sound as that, like an eagle soaring on the wind. The little ones are like a pair of butterflies in that harmony, all aflutter.

"Ain't that a sound." I twisted my neck about to catch a closer look.

The patroon chuckles. "The little one is a violin, the second is the viola, and the large one is the cello."

I turn about and face him, eye to eye. "Don't look too hard. Them ain't nothing but fancified fiddles. I can play them."

"I expect that is very true." He smiles. This patroon reminds me of a sidewinder, a peculiar sort of snake that saddles up to its prey sidewise. Then it smiles before it strikes.

I turn to watch the footman, still running ahead of the carriage.

"You city folk have a peculiar way of doing things, running when there's a perfectly fine carriage to ride in."

"You're a bit too free with your thoughts, petite River."

"None more than usual." I don't even crack a wise grin. Don't I know it, this highborn patroon knows them dandies on the dock. Them dandies had to know my da, because they knew Annie. My hackles rise. This here highborn patroon, this king of the city, I bet he knew Da.

Just then something roars, a fierce almighty roar that rips through the air. It ain't nothing I ever heard before. I jump about, standing in the carriage. There on the green are dandified

70

cages and large round platforms all draped in flags. There's dogs barking, and doves fluttering, and peacocks parading their large, fanlike tails.

And there I see a wonder cat the size of a pony, dressed in orange with black stripes. It roars again, showing teeth the size of my arms.

"That ain't natural." I shake my head. I can't tear my eyes away from it. "But ain't it a peculiar wonder."

"That, my dear," the patroon says, smiling, "is a tiger."

The cat walks slow, pacing back and forth in a cage as fancified as this carriage. His tail slashes through the air like lightning. People stare at the beastie: some laugh at it; one dares to throw a rock at it. And the big monster cat roars in a fitified rage.

There, too, in another cage I see a black bear cub walking in circles, swatting at rocks thrown at it. It rolls its head, a-bellowing its temper.

I turn about, facing forward now, eye to eye with the patroon. And I don't look away, either.

The patroon chuckles.

"You are very much like your papa."

I grin, perfectly pleased that I rile him. I grin him my grinniest grin. I can grin the bark off a tree if I mind to.

"I didn't mean it as a compliment worthy of a smile." His fingers tapdance on the handle of his cane. "I knew your papa for many years. He and I were—shall we say—business partners."

"I know my da's business partners. I ain't knowing you."

"Ah, petite River. But I know you! Your papa talked of you often. He called you stubborn, always moving too fast for your own good, more like rapids than the calmer waters of the delta. He called you his petite River."

The carriage follows the levee path along the big river. A breeze kicks up, freshening the smell. The patroon uses his cane to point to the street ahead. He smiles. "Rue Bourbon. Almost home."

On the corner stands a cottage set up against the street.

Black smoke belches out of its chimney, smelling like forge fires and iron. The sign hanging from the post says Laffite's Blacksmith Shop.

And now, don't I know this city patroon, at least by reputation. I should have seen this storm coming. This man here, he's Jean Laffite, the pirate patroon. Da told me about him. He's a slaver. Da says, the lowest form of humanity.

I ain't ever gave it much thought, how a human can own another. Not like Da, who thought it a special sort of hell and damnation. On the river there's only one boss—the patroon. Everyone's life depends on his way to steer through the current. Everyone heaves all the same, patroon and keeler. If they don't, everyone dies because death don't play favorites. When fortune comes, everyone earns the same share.

I must have looked like I seen some terrible wonder. Says him, "You know me."

"You be that slaver pirate Jean Laffite, right out of the Caribbean."

"Tsk-tsk." He smiles. "I am no pirate. I am a . . . corsair."

"A skunk can call itself a flower, but that don't make it so."

The pirate patroon chuckles as he lifts his cuff to his nose. Then he points to the market square. In a sweeping arc of his arm, he points to all them boodles of people walking about, selling and trading their wares. "Look out that way at all that you can see, petite River. Without me there would not be a bale of goods in the whole of market square."

I keep my eyes on the pirate patroon. I aim to take him head-on. "Da says them only the lowest of humanity, lower than a snake's belly, would sell another human."

Laffite throws one arm over his head, raising the brim of his hat. He chuckles. I can't tell if it's the sort that means he's about to tear my heart out.

"Well, here now!" He hoots. "I am being reprimanded by a river rat's pip who can't even comb her hair!"

The carriage pulls in front of the iron gates. It's a walled courtyard, flowers dripping over the top. And there, standing in front in a red dress bright as them flowers, pearls sparkling in the sun, is Annie Christmas.

And she ain't happy.

I lose all my whoop and sink low in the seat.

But Annie rushes to the black carriage following up behind us, right up to Cam. Others follow her, and together they ease him out of the carriage.

"Don't sit there aquiver." Jean Laffite chuckles. "Come now, come take your punishment as befitting the *fille* of Dan Fillian."

Chapter Seventeen

Gurdy hobbles from the carriage, his arms open wide. I wrap my arms around him but good, and together we walk through the iron gates.

Inside them flowered walls the cottage is as fine as I ever seen. Trees and bushes are all abloom, moss like an old man's beard hanging down from their branches. The house is the color of pink and yellow twilight.

And on the ironworks balcony stands a man, armed and ready and looking down on us. He ain't the only one watching. Another man walks up to Jean Laffite, greeting the pirate patroon with a hug and a kiss on each cheek. He's shorter, built like a barrel, and walks favoring one leg. But he smiles pretty. When he shouts, the very sky shakes. "Jean! I see you found the wayfarers without too much trouble?"

"Pierre!" says Jean Laffite. "Come meet our guests."

This man, Pierre, turns to me. One eye is crossed. I can't tell if he's looking at me or at Gurdy.

"Welcome to my home," he says. "I offer my deepest condolences for your papa. Nothing's more important than family."

And just then a woman walks up. Full in the family way, she is the same color of deep gold as her dress, all elegance, full of lace and finery. She waves her fan as she approaches, bowing her head to the pirate patroon. "Brother-in-law, I expect our guests are tired from their little adventure."

"Marie, sister." The pirate patroon bows. He kisses her on

both cheeks. Then he says, "I'll leave this petite River to your good graces. See if you can't do something with all that hair."

Marie turns to me. She looks me over, down to my toes, and then says, "My brother-in-law takes you under his protection. My purpose is to make you worthy of that kindness. It won't be easy, I declare"—she touches my hair, carefully as if she were touching a bee's nest—"but it's not impossible. I'm sure there's a *perle* under all that river mud. Catiche! Catiche, come help us."

A girl races up to her. She's a full head taller than myself, dressed in plain white linen. At first I think she's a slave. Da warned me about this confounded peculiarity to New Orleans, colored owning colored. But then the girl says, "Sister!"

Catiche and Marie hug as the younger turns toward me. This Catiche winces as if she ate some bug. "You call that hair?"

She's not willing to come too close, and she scowls all the more. But she takes me by the hand and pulls me down a path that disappears into flowery bushes. This ain't looking good for me, not at all. I begin to struggle against her grip, but she's as strong as any blacksmith.

"Stop being so wild, silly. It's only a bath!" says she.

"I ain't taking a bath!" I stand as tall as I might. But this Catiche pulls me behind the house to the kitchen shed. I growl almighty all the way to there.

"Sarah!" Catiche shouts as loud as any patroon. A big woman steps from the garden. Another turns, too, looking to Sarah and then to Catiche. "Sarah, I need your help making *this* presentable."

"I see to it, miss. We knew you were coming, river child. There's the bathing tub, all set up for you. Now, you drop your drawers." Sarah is as wide as Annie Christmas is tall. Something tells me she's just as ornery when her temper's up.

"I ain't." I shake my head. I cross my arms and dig my heels in.

"We knew that, too." She points to the other, who now jumps to, taking my shoulder. She and Catiche hold me down as Sarah pulls my britches off. Now Sarah takes a knife and comes at me. She steps up and goes for the spyglass strapped to my back. But now I fight them all harder. "I'm not afeared of none of you!"

"Wild child!" says Marie, stepping into the shed. She's raising her voice, but it's not a sharp call touched with anger. It's enough to quiet me down. "We are giving you a bath, not serving you up for dinner." She moves like a soft current as she takes the spyglass from my back. "My, this is a handsome case. I'll lay it here, always in your sight."

She gives a nod. Too late I discover I've been honeyfogled. Sarah lifts me straight off the ground as if I'm nothing but a twig. She sets me square in the barrel, and Catiche pours a bucket of water over me. Before I have a mind to swing about, Sarah pours a second bucket over my head.

And there I stand, in all my glory, soaked as any fish.

"Surely you are not afraid of a little water?" Marie smiles, kicking aside my clothes.

"I ain't afeared of nothing. I had a bath before." Da and Gurdy don't hold to the notion that baths spread the plague. "I just don't want one."

"Perhaps. But we're bigger than you are stubborn. So let's get you smelling better than that river." And she hands me a tub of soap. Real soap from across the seas, smelling like a field of flowers. Real quick I soap my belly. Marie points to my arms. I soap them up quick. She points to my legs, and I soap them, too.

Sarah takes a brush and scrubs my skin till it burns. "No more sass from you now, river child. I've more things to do than fight with some hobgoblin over a bath. How can it take three grown women to bathe one little pip?"

"She smells as bad as a skunk," Catiche says. "Can't rub that stink off. And look at all that hair."

I clench the rim of the barrel and clench my teeth as Catiche pours a pitcher of water over my head. Don't matter that the water's not that cold. In this swampy heat it ain't too bad. But I'm a fish in a barrel, and I don't like it.

Now Sarah rubs prettified oils through my tangle. Then she rubs my scalp until I think my eyes just might bounce right out of my head.

That moment three pips race into the kitchen, two boyos and a girl. The girl is half my size, and the boys even younger.

"Catherine! Hold your brothers now!" Marie says. "Don't let them get wet!"

"Look at all that red hair!" Catherine points. "*Oncle* says it's bad luck to have red hair."

I snarl like the tiger I seen. The little pip steps back in terror. Sarah smacks the back of my wet head. I yelp.

Just then the smaller of the boys slides through the mud, slamming into the barrel. He crumbles quickly and begins to bawl. Catherine gathers him up as Marie strokes his head. "Catherine, take them to your papa!"

Sarah dumps one last pitcher over my head and lifts me up. "Now, out of the barrel with you."

She takes a cloth to dry my hair, then tries to dry the rest of me, but I can't stand still for it. Then she holds up two tubes of cloth. They look like britches that're only half done.

"First, we make you respectable," says Sarah.

"I ain't respectable." I cross my arms, confused. "And I ain't putting on them silly things."

"Every young and proper lady needs"—now she whispers—"underdrawers. Step into them, and I'll show you how to tie them on."

"You ain't heard me." I stand my ground with a hard grin. "I ain't ever wore them things, and never will. You aiming for a fight about it?"

Just as quick, Catiche comes up behind me. "First the shift," she says as she pulls a sheet over my head with a huff. "Too much hair." Even as she succeeds getting it past my hair, I ain't able to take a breath before Marie slips another sheet over my head.

"The petticoat goes next." She hands me another fancified shift, with a lacy bottom. She ties up the back and then she spins me around and around, her fingers flying as she hooks the back.

She spins me around again and slips the dress over my head. It's the color of sunshine with vines of green leaves and pink flower buds.

"I look like a spring garden," I say, none too pleased.

"You look like a *petite fleur.*" Marie smiles. She pulls a comb through my tangle.

"She still smells," says Catiche.

I shoot her a prickly look.

"This ain't practical." I lift the skirts and wiggle my toes. Marie taps my chin to lift my head. As she braids my hair Sarah lifts my leg and slips on stockings, one foot at a time.

"Ain't ever seen feet as tiny as this on one so old. I don't think we have slippers this small. You'll have to wear your boots. Bijou, come here, silly girl! Brush them boots clean of the mud." Another girl pops her head up from a bushel of beans in the garden. This one is as tall as Catiche. Like them slaves in the market, she wears a dress of plain linen and a calico apron. She's a slave. Bijou disappears with my boots.

"How can you run in all this?" I ask Catiche.

"It's not proper for a young lady to run," she says.

"Ain't nothing proper about me." I scowl. The stockings itch, like there's a hill of ants crawling up and down my legs.

"Hold still now," says Marie. She finishes my hair, one large braid snaking down my back, tied at the end with a yellow ribbon. Finally, she returns the spy case to me, and Bijou returns with my boots. Now I smile at the sight of them. I don't mind that they're clean; they're mine. I hug them tight.

"You can take the rat out of the river," huffs Sarah, "but never the river out of the rat."

"Thank you, Sarah. You've worked wonders here." Marie holds a hand mirror up to me. "Now, tell me what you think."

I ain't ever seen myself this clean, and surely not so fancified. Ain't much to me, standing knee-high to a grasshopper, skin the color of peaches, with freckles that look like the Milky Way spilling across both cheeks. Despite Marie's attempt to tame my hair, dry wisps of it dance wildly. Eyes green as a spring leaf stare back at me. I ain't believing what I'm seeing. Some big sorrow suddenly swells inside my throat. It's hard to swallow, try as I might.

And I say, "You done civilized me."

Chapter Eighteen

The sun's fierce in the sky when I walk into the courtyard. I walk slow, unsteady in this dress. It wraps about my ankles. I keep pulling it free.

"Ain't you some!" a voice crows. I turn to Gurdy, sitting at a table. Ain't it happifying through and through to see him! I run up to him and hug him mightily again.

"There, there, little River." He's near to tears. "Your da be pleased."

And that's when I see them all. There's Cully, and Cay, and Chance, all of Annie's boyos, sitting near their brother Cam. And Cam's corned on rum: his smile is as crooked as his eyes. They're all laughing so hard, they're near to tears.

I step up to Cam, feeling powerful sorry for his hurt. I say, "Weren't my intention to get you hurt."

Cam smiles all the more. His hand waves as if he swats a fly. "Don't you worry none."

But Annie says—and it cracks like a whip—"Next time you're told to stay put, you stay put. Or I'll be the one cracking your lice."

The pirate patroon, Laffite, chuckles. He says, "Don't be harsh on the petite River, Annie Christmas. She thought her papa was in trouble. I admire her, *oui*. What would you have done if it were your son in danger?"

Pierre sits at a long table. And there's them dandies, Alaire and Alain from the docks, and they're all looking and laughing. Annie nods. "True enough. But that's my son that got his toe blown off. A mam can't see all that clear when it's one of her own." Now it's her sons, Chance and Cody and Coby, even Cully, too, who give a ripsnorting whoop at their brother's mishap.

"I can still dance, Ma. Ain't so bad!" Cam crows. "Besides, it ain't her that shot me."

"I've a mind about this Mother Colby. I plan to talk to her directly." Annie chuckles, wagging her head. She motions to me with open arms, and I hug her mightily. "Don't I see the error of my ways, making you keep to a promise you can't make."

That moment Catiche walks up carrying a tray of fruit and honey cakes. She sets it near them two dandies. She smiles honey sweet.

The three pips—Catherine, Jean Baptiste, and baby Martial—race from behind, nearly spinning me on my heels. They clamber like bees to honey, grabbing the cakes. Pierre Laffite laughs as baby Martial crawls up on his knees.

"And how's my namesake, the mighty Jean Baptiste?" Jean Laffite hoots as the elder toadie stands next to him.

"No worry yourself, little River," Gurdy whispers in my ear, tugging at my braid. "It a good moment here."

"Didn't mean for hurt to come to Cam." I shake my head. I take his hand, and he squeezes it mightily tight. "Gurdy, do you think Da is still out there?"

"I no say." Gurdy hugs me. "I do know, if anyone can escape that hellfire, it your da."

It gets me to thinking, and it gets me to hoping. Maybe Annie's right: maybe I need to sit still for a bit so I can start to see my way around the bend.

But it's hard to sit still when there's a thousand ants crawling up my legs. As the sun heats up, the itching turns to burning. Soon I can't sit still another moment.

Marie shoots me a prickly look. *Be still!*

But I ain't doing it no more.

I jump to and race down the path leading to the kitchen

shed where I can hear Sarah singing. Before I reach it, I jump under the bush and I crawl as far as I might. Quick, quick, I pull them stockings off. I bury them, too, in the back of them bushes. I smile as I put my boots back on, liking the fresh air.

It ain't civilized, don't I know it. But I ain't itching no more.

Chapter Nineteen

I ease next to Gurdy.

Jean Laffite is laughing. "I signed the letter, Agent of the Freebooters." He hoots, well pleased with himself.

But his brother Pierre ain't so pleased. He grumbles, "Brother, your taunting only feeds into the governor's suspicions."

"Nonsense. We are patriots, brother. We punish the British and the Spanish while doing our civic duty to provide goods in the open manner in which our business is done. That's what I wrote, nothing but the truth of it."

"We live in interesting times, *mon cher.*" Alain chuckles. "Those hawks in Congress are bent on war. Their dream of a grand America spreading from ocean to ocean, from the Gulf of Mexico to the North Pole, sways many a Southern 'gentleman.' "

Chance snorts. "Not everyone holds to that grand dream. Them Canadians ain't liking it none."

"Northerners ain't liking it a bit," adds Coffee. "Can't say them Shawnee be liking it, either."

Says Annie, easing back into her chair, her pearls shining in the sun, "Them codfish aristocrats in Congress seem bent on telling what can be traded and who can do the trading. But the best of us know the real business of living. So enough of this twaddle. Let's get on with it."

Jean Laffite puffs his cigar. "It will be our fortune if war comes our way. War will create shortages only we can supply. And every authority, including the governor, will be too distracted to pay any attention to our means of supplying their demands."

"Brother." Pierre leans forward. His wandering eye focuses on Laffite. "We're on the verge of financial ruin ourselves and cannot afford to have the governor look too closely into our affairs. You risk everything for your pride."

"My dear brother"—Jean Laffite puffs his cigar—"I won't let that happen. Have you not learned by now, I always have a plan. So have a toast to our new partner, Annie Christmas."

Annie says, "Give me your hand on it, and it's a deal we have!"

It can't be true, but my ears are hearing it so! Annie Christmas partners with the devils themselves, them Laffite pirates? Is Annie to become a slave trader, too?

I look to Gurdy, and he squeezes my hand. He's a-smiling, but he's hiding something behind it. If Da were here, he'd have a say into this, for sure. Something's astir, all right. I see more trouble coming.

At least now it ain't me bringing it.

Chapter Twenty

Long before the twilight fades into night, Annie and her boyos leave, taking a wagon of supplies and Cam back to the *Big River's Daughter*. Cam's singing loud as he might, a warbling that any bird would be shamed to let loose.

"You promise me, you stay put. No looking for your da. You safe here," says Gurdy. He sits on the back edge of the wagon and gives me a nod. He ain't saying good-bye, he said, but there's things to be done on the boat. Don't worry, all's well.

Ain't one word spoke about what's a-coming.

I watch the wagon roll down the street. I promised I'd stay put. But there's a twitch of sorrow seeing them go. We said our quick good-byes. Annie told me to stand tall, like Da would've wanted. He'd be proud of me, said she. But, she ain't asked me to come on the river. Maybe she thinks I don't belong there no more. Maybe she thinks I need to stay away till I find my sea legs again. But it ain't Annie's place to tell me what I need.

And ain't that the truth of it—she never even asked me.

"Don't worry." Catiche creeps up from behind, like a cat stepping out of the shadows. "Oncle says your man, Gurdy, belongs on the boat, not here."

"Gurdy don't belong to no one," I say, vexed. "But he does belong on a boat."

Catiche smiles as she pulls me into the courtyard. "Come along now. No more fretting. Oncle has a surprise for us!"

We walk into the courtyard, to the grand porch behind the

house. Sitting beside Jean Laffite is his brother, still scowling. But the three pips watch me quietlike, as if I'm about to give them a honey cake. Laffite smiles. "Ah, petite River!"

Marie steps up, and she's all a-smile, too. She hands the pirate patroon a long wooden box made with deep dark wood ashine in the glow of a lantern.

"As I recall from our buggy ride, you boast that you can play a fiddle," he says. "I've no doubt the fille of Dan Fillian aims to make good on that boast, oui?" He opens the box, and then holds up the finest fiddle I ever seen. There's narry a scratch on its shiny dark wood. He offers it to me.

Don't I know, it's taking from the devil himself, and there's always a price to pay for such a gift. But Annie Christmas left me behind, and ain't no one here has my back. Until I have a plan, I aim to stay alive. So I take that fancy fiddle. And it's a perfect melody just to look at.

"So, petite River, make good on your boast." The pirate patroon lights a cigar, easing into his big chair.

I stand in the middle of the grand porch and look about. Fireflies bounce off the flowering bushes. There's humming from them rainbow birds dipping into the red blossoms and chirrups as birds blend in near harmony with the chirr of cicadas and crickets. Church bells chime in the distance.

I remember a song from a long time past, one Da sang as we watched the sun set, the last light flickering soft on the big river. An osprey floated with outstretched wings above us.

"That's Ma." Da had pointed to the light. "That soft flicker of light easing us home. And that big ol' bird, see how he plays on the wind, following the light?"

Then Da sang to me about home on the big river.

In that tick in time, I'm on the *Molly Dear*, sitting with Da on the bow. There's Gurdy on the steering oar. Curt stands on the cabin of his *Lady Twilight* watching the current. And that big ol' bird follows the river of light flickering on the waves, swooping and playing in his freedom.

I bring this fancy fiddle under my chin. The strings feel like the finest spun silk a spider might envy. And I let my old sorrow sail through my fingers, spilling onto that fancified fiddle.

When I look up, I see tears aflow on Marie's cheeks as she brings close her three pips. Catiche is a-smiling and crying at once. Pierre Laffite is watching me, too, his scowl a little less fierce. There ain't no tears flowing from his crooked eye, but he's remembering some day long ago.

And the pirate patroon himself, Jean Laffite, nods and smiles.

Don't I know, too, I ain't got time to think on about what I don't got. Better to think what comes next.

So now I play a new tune, a dancing tune, and soon enough the three pips are gallivanting about, and Marie and Pierre are clapping. Catiche joins the dance as the last of the twilight falls.

Chapter Twenty-One

The clean sheets smell like flowers, and for the first time in days, my belly is full. But it ain't enough to ease my dreams. I sleep in fits, that big river chasing me down. I'm glad for the morning when it finally comes.

I'm hoping Gurdy gets here soon to give me the all's well, or Annie Christmas, to take me aboard.

But it's Catiche that meets me at dawnlight.

She bursts into the room. "Dress now, sleepyhead!" She sings more than talks. "Oncle has given us a carriage, and Miss Grace will accompany us to the dress shop."

"Miss Grace?" I ain't met her.

"She's my nurse, silly," Catiche sings more. "Madame Rochon is meeting us directly. How delightful! We're to pick the material for my dress. My debut comes with the October ball, and there's much to do until then! Come along! It'll be such an adventure!"

"Madame Rochon?"

"Marie is working with the very important Madame Rochon to find me a strong arrangement. You'll meet her at the shop! She's very very important, and very wealthy, you know. She owns many very fine properties and grocery stores. Her son is an important man in the government in Haiti. She and Oncle are business partners now. So you must be on your best behavior!"

She continues to sing as she helps me pull down the layers of the dress. She stops suddenlike, and looks at me square, like she swallowed a handful of slugs.

"Where are your stockings?" says she.

"Can't say that I know." I shrug. If I say I took them off, she'll crack my lice. So I ain't saying.

"Well, that's just . . ." She shakes her head in disapproval.

"Don't worry none. Ain't no one going to know unless they look under my dress. And they do that, I'll lick 'em but good." I smile as I slip into my boots.

I reach for the spyglass and ease it over my shoulder.

Catiche clears her throat and curls her lip up. For sure she'll bite it off in her disapproval. I tighten the strap and give a nod. I ain't taking it off.

She heaves a sigh, knowing when to give up.

"Come along, then." She pulls me to the dining room.

The house is in a-flurry, like a keeler on a wild current. Marie is calling orders to Sarah, who is calling orders to Bijou, who is bringing platters of fruit and bread to a big table in the courtyard. Ain't a keeler patroon that runs a ship as tight as that Marie. Except Da.

There sit the brother pirates Laffite. Other river rats are sitting with them, but none that I know. Alain and Alaire are there, too, swapping howdies with the pirates like old friends.

But I don't see Annie Christmas or Gurdy.

Marie pushes us to the back courtyard, where the three pips run about in the yard under the watchful eyes of Sarah.

Miss Grace gives me a wary eye. She ain't much bigger than Catiche, but she ain't no sapling. Dressed in deep green and lace, she wears a bonnet topped with white feathers. Them feathers floating in the air stand near as high as she is tall. She scowls her disapproval when she looks at me. Something tells me her bite is just as mean.

They don't like me being here any more than I like being here. But for some reason they're holding their tongues.

Even before I finish my breakfast bread, Miss Grace pushes me and Catiche to a carriage waiting on the street. A man stands on the back of the seat, armed and ready. He tips his hat as I step into the carriage. And he winks at my boots.

"Them nice boots," he says.

"Ain't them shiny as sunlight!" I say.

Miss Grace clears her throat. And I sit.

"What is a day-byu dress?" I ask Catiche.

"It's the perfect dress for the finest ball. Come fall, I am making my debut," Catiche rolls in her laughter. "When I make my entrance at the debut, I'll be a full woman, and ready to be a *placée*."

"Don't you already know your place?" I'm all befuddled now. Cully had warned me of the city's vexing ways to put everyone in their proper place.

"A placée." Catiche chuckles. And then says she, "You hear me well, River Fillian. You behave, or Oncle will deal with you outright."

I'm starting to see around the bend now. These here city folk may not like me none, but they dare not go against the pirate patroon, because he sees some value in me. But it ain't personal value. It's because I'm the pip of Dan Fillian, and he thinks I'll tell him something about Da's trade routes.

The carriage pulls up to a storefront. Catiche finds her smile again. She waves to the two women standing just outside the front door. One is a tall woman the color of deep tea, her hair bundled in a bright turban. The other also wears a hat crowned with sweeping white feathers, but her feathers are much more grand. No doubt, here stands Madame Rochon. She carries a cane, just like the pirate patroon. Sure enough, she looks like a queen, standing with her gloved hands crossed in front of her.

The turbaned woman waves back to Catiche as the carriage rolls up. "There you are, you beautiful flower. You will be the talk of the town, I promise you!"

Catiche floats off the carriage and turns to Madame Rochon. Before she offers any word, she curtsies. Miss Grace's scowl finally breaks with an unexpected smile, then the feathers in her hat sweep low, all atremble as she curtsies back. The turbaned woman rushes up, embracing Catiche and then embracing Miss Grace. I stand there watching them swap howdies until they finally notice me. Catiche arches one of her brows. She ain't saying what she's expecting me to do. I expect she's expecting me to curtsy all the same.

"Howdy," I say, placing one boot behind the other. I scoop. I ain't ever curtsied before, and I wobble in my scooping.

The turbaned woman turns to me, smiling, "And who is this little hobgoblin? Does she need a dress, too?"

"Not me!" I say, digging my heels in. "I don't need a day-byu."

The coachman chuckles. Miss Grace shoots him a prickly look, and he turns about.

"She's Oncle's new charge," Catiche explains.

"She's a savage," hisses Miss Grace.

"Oncle likes her," Catiche insists. It's like I'm not even there. "He says we must feel charity toward those deserving."

"Well then, are you sure you do not want a dress? We can dress you like a princess!" The turbaned woman smiles down at me.

"I ain't much a princess," I say.

"Madame Rochon!" Catiche swirls and begins to sing again. "This is *such* an honor. I cannot thank you enough for such a courtesy. And Miss Pearl, I have all faith that you'll make the grandest dress, perhaps a fine green silk to bring out my eyes! Everyone will be so jealous!"

Catiche and Miss Pearl talk so fast, it sounds like too many bees stuffed in a hive. They swoon over the rainbow colors of all them clothes. Miss Grace nods her approval of the green silk. Ain't no way she can get a word in sideways with all that buzzing.

Madame Rochon sits next to me and, without turning her head, says, "So, you are Jean Laffite's new pet."

"I don't think so," I say, not turning my head, either. "Unless you're meaning I'm visiting."

"Yes." She chuckles. Now she looks my way. "That's exactly what I mean. I suppose this means you are a friend of Annie Christmas as well?"

Now I look at her square. "You friends with Annie, too?"

"At one time, many years ago." Madame Rochon nods her approval to Catiche and Miss Pearl as they hold up a shimmering cloth. But she says to me, "We were the best of friends, more like sisters really."

"Then you had a rough-and-tumble." I nod in understanding.

"That's how it always ends. Prolly a big rough-and-tumble, leaving no room left for a handshake."

"Yes, that's exactly what I mean. We had a rough-and-tumble over how certain things should be done. Annie doesn't like to be told how to live her life."

"You ain't lost a pearl, did you?"

"No, just a friendship," says she. "Sometimes that's more valuable than a mere pearl. Are you sure you don't need a dress? Or perhaps slippers?"

"I ain't needing a dress, and my boots suit me well enough," I say. "Don't you worry none. I already know my place."

"Your place?" Madame Rochon puckers her lips in befuddlement. Then she cracks a smile. "Ah, you speak of Catiche's plaçage—she'll have a protector, a provider."

"You looking to marry Catiche off?"

"No, my dear little vulgar hobgoblin. The truth of the matter, not everyone can be the free spirit that becomes Annie Christmas or live like a hobgoblin on a boat. Some of us have very few choices in life. So we make the best of what we have. We create our own success."

She's quiet for a moment, like she's considering her next words with special care. And then says she, "You understand, yes? We can't allow Catiche to marry someone beneath her station and live a life in poverty and drudgery. And it's against the law for a woman of color to marry a white man. So we use the honorable and ancient tradition of plaçage. We call it *marriage de la main gauche*." Madame Rochon chuckles. "I was placée to a wealthy man and am now very rich because I was smart about the arrangement. I arranged for Marie to become placée with Pierre Laffite, and see how well it has worked for both of them? Now I help Marie find a suitable arrangement for Catiche: a Catholic, of course, and wealthy to support her and their children. If she's smart enough, and certainly she is, she'll become wealthy in her own right. She'll own properties, and perhaps a store, and certainly her own home. Her sons will be educated in the finest schools in France. Her daughters, well, daughters

91

grow up to be placées or they go to the convent. At least this way she has a choice in her arrangements."

Just then Catiche squeals. I jump to, but she ain't squealing out of fear. She's clapping her hands, smiling to beat the sunshine.

"Here, child!" Madame Rochon leaves her seat to take a closer look at the cloth. "Lovely, my dear! Just like you!"

Well, there you are, and there you ain't. Don't I see it straight now? Mother Colby and them look mightily downtrodden in the Sure Enuf. But ain't it a cage no different from this fancified one? I'm thinking, this is why Annie ran to the river, just like Da ran to the river—to find their own place.

That big Mississip, Da said, she ain't easy. That river ain't easy at all. But she ain't no cage.

I sit in a corner. There's more color on these shelves than any field of spring flowers across a swampy prairie. My fingers walk across the many silks, and each feels smooth as any flower petal. Shelf after shelf, the colors are all ashiny and bright.

Just then I see a slender tail whip through a loose flap on the corner of one fold. It got caught in them folds, and now it's trying to get free. Looks like another river rat found its way where it don't belong.

Well, ain't this some? My own smile twitches as I look for a way to chase it down.

I need something long, something to help this critter turn its direction. But all I have is my spyglass.

I glance over my shoulder to make sure no one is watching. Catiche and Miss Pearl are all abuzz as ever. Madame Rochon is gathering lace, wrapping Catiche in various trims. And Miss Grace has all eyes on Catiche.

Even the guard stands with his back to the door.

Slipping the spy case from my back, I tap the twitch. The rat squeaks, turns, and scampers closer to the wall, finally freeing itself from the cloth.

And there it stands, twitching its whiskers. It ain't afeard. In fact, it's downright bold. A big brown betty, so big and mean-like, it could take on any cat and probably win.

I nudge it again with my spy case. It turns about so quickly, I jump back, dropping my case. In that tick of time, the rat twists, running through the strap, tetchy as a teased snake. The strap tangles in its hind feet, and that tetched rat begins dragging my case, not slowing down a tickle.

Miss Grace shrieks. But it's Miss Pearl that jumps into action. She grabs a broom and swings it mightily as she chases after that rat.

"Damnable rats! Every ship brings in a new crop. It's worse than pickpockets!"

I jump to and chase it down, too, pulling the cloth free of the shelves so it ain't got a place to hide. But that critter is fast. I jump and flip to keep up with it. I jump too far and smash into a shelf. All suddenlike, the shelf topples. Madame Rochon swirls about, stunned. Miss Pearl shouts, "No! You hooligan!"

Right then Catiche sees the rat. She lets loose such a screech, it's likely to burst the glass window. The guard rushes inside, his pistol cocked and ready. The rat jumps and turns about, coming my way.

I leap after the rat, catching the case and snatching it free. That rat spins hard about, its tail whipping like a twirligig.

And that's when the real trouble begins. As it lands near Madame Rochon she screams, throwing her hat and a-stomping after the rat. Miss Pearl swoops with the broom. The world explodes in that moment as Catiche screeches again, trying to jump out of the way. But she jumps so high that she rips the fine blue silk cloth. The guard points his gun at the rat as if about to fire when Miss Grace jumps in front of the screaming girl. She waves her arms like a flag, as if the man might shoot Catiche. They both turn white as cotton, screaming, "No! No!"

Before Miss Pearl turns that broom on me, and before Miss Grace rips my ear off, I hightail it out the door, Da's spy case in hand. Outside now, I weave past the boodle of people gathering at the window to see what the ruckus is all about.

I escaped the cage and feel like hooting! The rat, on the other hand, is a goner for sure.

And that's when I hear it across the way, that fearsome roar.

Chapter Twenty-Two

I run like a deer across a meadow. I jump across the ditch, near tripping over the dress wrapping around my legs. Don't I know it, dresses are evil things, and less than useful, like legs on a fish. I'd rip it right off if I could. Instead, I pull it up, stuffing the ends in my sash, and hop-jump-run across the street and into the square. No one pays notice to this here river rat.

Some gather on the green, taking in the cool morning air before the sun grows fierce. Street callers call out wares to sell: Peaches! Bananas! Honey cakes!

Right then another roar rips through the air. Ain't ever heard such a sad sound in all my years.

Not one head turns in that direction.

But I look.

I follow the roaring to the cages on the green, all lined up like a row of shops. And inside are all manner of pitiful critters. There's a black bear a-huddle in the corner of his cage wailing like a cub crying for its ma. There's coons chittering to the sky. There's a pair of gators hissing and snapping at the air. And a snake as thick as my own waist lies still as stone. It could swallow me whole if it had a mind to.

Roaming the muddy green are peacocks, with their prettified feathers, shrieking like sirens. Roosters and chickens are a-crowing and clucking. There's geese, and doves, and a donkey, too. An elephant is roped to a pole, shaking its head.

There in the last cage stands the tiger. That's what the patroon called it. Ain't that big cat some! But even I can tell it but a young'un, for its feet seem too big for them legs. It roars so fearsome, the air rips with anger and hate.

But just as loud are the screams of delight from a boodle of boys surrounding the cage.

Quick I duck behind a tree. One boy stands two heads taller than me, his hair the color of ripe bananas. He's dressed in the trousers of an aristocrat. He throws a big rounder, striking the cat in its haunches.

The cat, with its ears flattened and teeth bared, roars back. It's a mighty roar, and it bats at them cage bars as if it hopes to break them. Despite its mighty roar that tiger's a pitiable sight. Its fur stands ragged and mangy, its ribs poking out. But it ain't backing into some corner. It stands its ground against the dandified codfish.

Da didn't like cats, calling them little devils with their own mind about how life works. But I'm thinking, it don't seem fair to pitch a rock against something that can't fight back. I expect it's up to me to champion that cat.

I look for a proper rounder, something hard to get the attention of that codfish. There ain't a good rounder to be found, but there's plenty of peaches. It ain't hard pinching some good ones from the baskets.

I throw the first, hard as Da threw the rounders across the river. And I hit the boy right atop his banana-color hair. The boy shrieks as wild and woolly as a polecat that got its tail twisted in a knot. Before he's a chance to look around to see who dared kick his lice, I throw another peach. Just that fast, I pitch the third. Both times I hit him on his back. The boy shrieks louder in fright, and the whole boodle set out a-running.

I look around, careful them boyos don't return, then I walk up to the tiger in the cage. The tiger roars at me. He's thinking I'm going to hurt him, too. But I just look at him. For as big as he is, he's still a cub, too young to be without his ma. His fur is orange-and-black stripes set against white fur on his stomach. But that whiteness is dull with mud and bugs and other filth from his life spent in a cage. He's fierce and angry at the world, batting at the bars.

Don't I know how it is to carry such a terrible heavy, anger. It weighs so heavy it hurts all over.

"Careful, petite River." A familiar voice chuckles behind me. "That little kitty will eat you."

"He's just angry," I say.

"Mister Laffite!"

We both swerve at the new voice.

"Them boys are brutish spoiled rats. I've been after them and after them to leave my babies alone. Thank you for chasing them away. Maybe now they will!" He's a skinny rail of a man, bent over like a sapling in a strong wind. He points to the tiger. "Ain't he a beaut? Caught him meself while on safari in India. Me and the maharagee himself went on the tiger hunt, killed his big mam. He'll be the center of attraction, he will. If the tiger beats the bear, he'll fight the bull soon enough. If the bull wins, several pieces of fireworks will be attached to his back to produce a very entertaining amusement, dare I say. Care to place your bets now?" He points to a large striped skin spread out across another cage. "That's his mam."

I shake my head in pure sorrow for the cat. I say, "He don't look fully grown."

"Not even a year, and look how big he is. When he's totally growed, he'll be the size of a horse. Won't he be some, a real king of the forest!"

"A fine specimen at that." Laffite tips his hat. His fingers are all a-twitch. He's wanting to move out of here.

"Yes, yes! But wait till you see them other jewels!" The man speaks so fast, it's like he's talking three tales at once. "There's a donkey, a special one of a kind. She sings, you know, a true wonder of wonders!"

Laffite clears his throat, making it rattle like thunder. "You'll excuse us, but I have a pressing engagement." Laffite backs away, tipping his hat. That snake-oil man don't stop talking, telling us of all them wonders: a snake that ate a cow, the biggest rooster this side of the Mississip, the goose that laid the golden egg. Laffite don't stop backing away. He uses his cane to push me along.

That big, ragged cat hisses behind them bars. He don't belong here, and he knows it. He's like me, in a place he don't belong but ain't got no other place to go.

At least that big cat ain't backing down. He ain't giving up.

I hang my head, eyeing my prettified dress. I glance back at that tiger sitting there in his fancified cage. "He looks all full of sorrow."

"What sorrow can he have?" Laffite huffs. "Everything he might ever need is provided for him." He opens the carriage door for me, and the coachman tips his hat. "I, on the other hand, have many worries. I have a business meeting with a financier, to discuss opportunities to expand my trade on the river. I didn't expect to see such a petite River throwing peaches."

Ahead I see that the storefront has cleared. I wonder if Catiche has already gone home. And it hits me like a peach to my own noggin, how *did* Laffite find me so quickly?

"Just so you know," I say. "No matter how nice you are, I won't say one word about Da's trading routes."

"You do me a great injustice, River. It's my Christian duty to look after a child in need." He's smiling at me, but it's a crooked smile. One of them hidey smiles. His fingers tap the end of his cane, and his green eyes turn dark, drilling me like an eagle's stare. "No apologies, petite River?"

"Ain't got nothing to be sorry for. That codfish ain't nothing more than a goosey coward, throwing rocks at something that can't get out of the way."

"I'm not talking about the tiger, River. I'm sure those boys had it coming. I'm talking about the events in the store . . . with a rat?"

"That rat got something that belonged to me," I say. "Had to get back what's mine."

"I can't argue with that. One has the right to protect his property. But Catiche is upset. And Miss Grace is in a temper, which will send Marie into a fit. I'm not looking forward to facing that storm when we get home. And I need from you something to aid me in that battle. Such as an apology."

"True enough, you're in a pickle." I nod in agreement. "But I ain't got no say over the goings-on with a rat."

It seems a short tick in time before the carriage pulls in front of the courtyard. The first carriage, carrying Catiche, has already parked, and she is wailing in her worry about a dress. Miss Grace is holding her shoulders, patting her arm. Miss Grace shoots a look in my direction, surely vexed with me. Then the two of them leave the carriage and disappear into the courtyard.

The coachman opens the door of our carriage, but the pirate patroon ain't moving. His fingers tap faster on his cane. He looks to the courtyard, then to me. His brow twitches in a worm of worry.

"You'd best untuck your dress," he says, tapping his cane. Still he ain't moving. Whatever's waiting beyond that wall is fierce, I expect.

I'm still smiling as I smooth out the dress, making it all properlike. "Don't seem right that a pirate patroon be so afeared of a girl."

"No," he says, "it don't seem right at all." He still ain't moving.

So I ain't moving.

After another moment he says, "You know, it's proper for a young miss to exit the carriage first."

"Prolly. But I ain't proper," I say. "But if you be so afeared, I'll surely go first."

"I'll go, sir." The coachman chuckles. "I'm armed."

Right then Pierre Laffite rushes out of the courtyard. And he done turn as white as a ghost.

"Jean! Hurry along, Jean! It's the talk of the town already. This little whelp attacked the Dubois son—"

"I did not!" I straighten my back, sitting tall as I might. I'm feeling quite vexed myself. "I ain't attack that codfish. I hit him with a peach. The most I did is dirty his britches, and maybe dampen his prettified hair."

Jean Laffite looks at me with a huff. Then he says in one of them long, low whispers, "I have a hundred men working for me, all jumping at the sound of my voice. Some of them are as mean as any wildcat. But not a one is as much trouble as you."

Now I smile pretty, quite taken with myself. "That's me. Always at the ready, Da says."

Pierre Laffite shoots me a sharp glance. "Catiche's fabric is in ruins. Marie is in an uproar, still vexed about not leaving for the summer, fearing the yellow fever. Miss Grace, well, there's a storm that won't be calmed. Both are fretting that Madame Rochon will back out of our agreement to help Catiche."

"Come down, Jean! I won't go back without you!"

"Worry not, brother." Jean Laffite finally stands up. "Madame Rochon knows a good deal when she hears one. That's how she became rich." He turns to me and sighs so heavy, I'm almost sorry for him.

Almost.

I smile at the pirate patroon. "Yup, you surely are swimming in a barrel of pickles now."

"You'll want to wash up before meeting with Marie." He points to the end of the wall. "I'm sure Sarah will have a bucket of wash water waiting. Once you're done, come find me."

Laffite looks at the house and heaves a big, shoulder-sagging sigh. Only then does he step out of the carriage. He adjusts his hat before stepping through the iron gates. Don't you know it, I smile hearing Catiche wailing anew. I walk slowly through the side gate, pretty as I please. I aim to take my time. All day long if need be.

I find Sarah working on the big fire, the smells of the gumbo roux drifting with the smoke. She and Bijou are cooking outside. Them are singing, too, and it ain't so bad. They almost drown out the wailing in the big house. Running about the shed are the three pips.

Sarah sees me coming, and she laughs hearty.

"Well now, here's a sight! I was thinking the three little ones would need a washup before you, but I see I'm wrong! Well, don't just stand there. Take off the dress, and let's see what we can do with it." Sarah's hands dance through the laces on the dress. In no time it's off, and who-op! I can breathe again. I inhale a deep, filling breath.

Sarah hands it to Bijou, who takes the dress and runs off toward the house.

"You know, it isn't ladylike to go without stockings," says Sarah, her eyebrows as pointed as her smile.

"I expect not," I say.

"Well, come along now. While we wait for Bijou to find you a dress you can stand here and watch my roux." Sarah laughs, now standing over a big pot. She adds a handful of flour to some fat. "How can something so little as you cause such a big stir?"

It can take hours to cook up a good gumbo. Some days when the *Molly Dear* moored for repairs, and not a tavern in sight, Gurdy stirred up a big pot for the brigade. I breathe in them smells of smoke and onion thinking of Gurdy's cooking. I must have been looking like some because Sarah chuckles. She chops the okra with the same menace as Gurdy wielding Big Sally. With the same twisting wrist, she scoops the okra up, slime dripping like long webs, and pours it into the roux.

"Stir it slow, and don't let it burn," says she. "Next time you have a need to go after that Dubois boy, use an onion instead of a peach. That smell will follow him around for days."

I'm hoping Bijou takes her time. I don't mind standing here. It's getting hot, true enough, hot enough that skeeters run for shade. But for sure, it's cooler here than in that house.

Chapter Twenty-Three

All too fast, Bijou returns with a dress. It's green as new leaves, or more like them inchy worms that chew on sprigs. I groan as she helps me into it, and now . . . don't I know what comes next. My legs feel heavy and unmoving as stone.

Says Bijou, "I'm not wanting to be you right now."

"You go along, river child." Sarah pushes me on. "If they get on you too much, you're more than welcome to help us out here."

I had promised Gurdy to stay put, but it's getting mighty hard to see the sense of it. Why don't they come back for me? I ain't running to that big house. I ain't in a hurry to catch an earful from Catiche or Miss Grace. So I slog to the house like I'm slogging through the muddy river. As I get closer, I don't hear any shouting, not even a wail. I'm hoping the anger's done.

But then I hear voices. It's an ominous talk, like Da held just before a raid. I walk even slower, hiding in the shadows behind flowering bushes.

Miss Grace is still in a temper, but she's hissing now. She's trying to keep her voice low. It seems a struggle for her to keep calm. "She is a savage, Mister Laffite. Catiche's reputation is ruined."

"I try to be charitable, Jean," Marie says with a huff. "But she caused such a scene at the shop. How will that affect your business with Madame Rochon?"

"I do not think my business partners will be swayed by an affray with a rat in a dress shop, Marie." Jean starts to chuckle, but suddenly he swallows it. Then he raises his voice. "What would you have me do?"

If my da had raised his voice like that, every man best back down quick or expect a good licking. But Marie and Miss Grace, they don't.

"A savage, vulgar offspring of a river rat," Miss Grace hisses with more venom. She'd put a rattler to shame, true enough.

Da weren't just any river rat! He was the best of them, the king of the river! I should walk onto that porch, let them all have a piece of my temper.

Instead, I stoop low in the shadow, ears to the wind.

"Dan Fillian wasn't just any river rat, Miss Grace. He was not just another pirate. In fact, some would say he was the most powerful patroon on the river." Laffite taps his cane. "Catiche, you will have your dress, and you will attend the grand ball and make your debut. But all this takes money. And for that, remember she's the fille of Dan Fillian, and now the surviving partner to Annie Christmas. She's key to a fortune, I tell you."

"Are times that desperate, brother"—Marie's voice trembles with worry—"that we must have that . . . wild thing . . . live with us?"

"Calm yourself, Marie." Pierre speaks up. "Or you'll have that babe right now."

"I'll not lie to you, Marie," the pirate patroon says. "We've had better days." They quiet, each eaten by their own worms of worry. The pirate patroon paces, tapping his cane. After a long moment he says, "So each of you will do your part."

I should have listened to Cully. These toadies wouldn't look my way at all except now they need me. They think I can bring them a fortune. But that pirate aims to steal from my da, from me. Then I suspect he plans to do away with me.

I aim to escape this cage, somehow.

I walk into the courtyard. The pirate patroon turns on his heels with a smile. "Much better, petite River!" Even Marie and Catiche smile. Miss Grace is still scowling, but she says not a word.

"I ain't heard from Annie and Gurdy," I say.

"My apologies, petite River. Annie sent a message, and in all the excitement I neglected my duty to pass it on to you. Repairs on the boat are taking a bit longer than expected. But they remain concerned for your safety and wish you to continue to enjoy your stay."

"What do you mean, concerned for my safety? I can take care of myself," I say.

"You'll remember Hogg Tyler and Mother Colby? Well, petite River, they're in an uproar over Annie and her sons. They have vowed your demise as a way to get to Annie. I can protect you from those villains as long as you remain under my protection. Annie will send word as soon as she's done. So while we wait, we enjoy your company."

I see it plain now. He's lying to me. Maybe from the very start. I sit on the porch, slipping behind them others. I look in the direction of the big river. Something don't smell right, and it's more than city stink. Annie may consider leaving me behind, but Gurdy would never allow it—no matter what this patroon says.

Catiche and Marie continue to discuss her dress while the pirates discuss their business in low whispers. The midday sun rises, and so does its heat. The pips and their mam lie down to rest. Catiche disappears, too, then even that pirate patroon himself begs his leave.

The house goes quiet.

And now it's my chance. I aim to see Annie, tell her about my suspicions. Then I'll stay put on that boat. I don't even pack my belongings. I got Da's spy case on my back, got my boots—that's all I need. I head back to the kitchen house.

Hanging for the morrow's meal is a chicken, feathers still intact.

I run right through the side entrance, down the street, and to the green. I run like the devil itself is on my tail.

There's hardly a soul about, not a man or skeeter buzz in the heat-heavy air. But there's a rabble enough in every tavern and corner café. When I get to the green, I see them caged animals heaving in the heat. The tiger lies still, but he's awake, watching me come toward him.

I unwrap my skirt and show him the chicken, slipping what I can through them bars. The tiger jumps, baring his teeth. He ain't having an easy go of it. But he uses his claws and teeth to get the carcass inside.

"Ain't right you being here," I whisper. That big cat shakes the bird, feathers flying everywhere. He rips it apart and swallows it.

I say, "Just so you know, if I could, I'd let you free."

Then I shoot off like a bullet, right to the docks. The closer I get to the river, the faster I go. I can smell it now, fish and smoky black earth of river mud tangled with the salty smell of the sea. But when I reach the levee, I stop sudden, like a stone done struck me hard.

I can't see her, not anywhere on the dock. The *Big River's Daughter*, she's gone!

And that old anger rushes brand new again. I run down the dock as far as I might, hoping to see that keeler. I reach the very edge, and there, the big river stretches way out in front of me. She's calm and gentle, like she was that day before the earth tore itself apart. There's an osprey, too, crying in the flickering red light on the horizon.

It ain't an easy life, Da said, not for the weak-bodied or the weak-hearted. But for those of us who be her sons and daughters, ain't no other place we call home. Telling a river rat not to be on the water, well, that's like telling water not to be wet.

"You bully river! You know who this is?" I shout to the river, shouting so loud, the osprey retreats to the treetops, a-shrieking its rage. "You know my da! Now you get to know me! I'm the same rough-and-tumble, no-holds-barred. So do your best, you big bully river. You ain't beat me down! I'm here to stay!"

I fall to my knees, all a-shivering in my tears. Sorrow overtakes my anger in a powerful wave. "You hear me, you bloody river? You ain't leaving me so easy!"

But they did, Annie and her boyos. And Gurdy. Just like that, they left me.

Chapter Twenty-Four

I'm all atremble when I walk back to the tiger's cage. He's sleeping now, but opens one eye when he hears me coming.

"Seems like we're the same." I sit, the sorrow too heavy to carry. I ain't got no choice but to head back to that pirate Jean Laffite. That buzzard lied about hearing from Annie. No telling what else he lied about. Maybe he told Annie some story about me? Maybe he convinced her that I wanted to stay with him?

But Annie would still have said good-bye. Gurdy would have said good-bye.

Unless the story he told was so terrible, they didn't want to see me again.

By the time I walk into the courtyard, the family is just beginning to stir. I sit in the garden till they find me. First, the pips run up, playing, laughing, shrieking, "Here! Here!"

Then, the pirate rushes out, followed by Marie and Catiche.

Marie stops, pointing to my dress, stained with mud from the docks, blood from the chicken. "You ruin another dress? Child, whatever did you do?"

"Calm yourself, sister. We're glad you are safe, petite River! Change your dress, then delight us with more music!" He smiles pretty as he hands me the fancy fiddle. I almost believe he's glad to see me, he lies that good.

And so I play. Them pips dance, and that pirate patroon, he winks at me.

He thinks I know my place now.

He's right. But it ain't in this fancy cage, and not in this civilized city.

Chapter Twenty-Five

Da once told me as he was teaching me to use the spyglass, you need to see your way around a bend before steering the boat ahead. Need to look from shore to shore to see how the water's moving, look at them eddies in the waves to see where shallows lie, look at the surface to see how the wind blows. Says Da, you can't figure out how to move ahead without knowing the full story of where you are.

The morning next, long before the sun comes up, long before even Sarah wakes up, I pinch another chicken. Dawnlight is a pink sliver across the horizon, and the candles that light the streetlamps still burn bright. The lamplighter is making his way down the avenue to put them out. Soon enough this city will wake up.

I aim to figure out why Annie left without me. Gurdy wouldn't leave me unless he had no choice. And he wouldn't leave me unless he thought I'd be safe with Jean Laffite. That pirate lied to them, too. I know it.

Annie Christmas was always swapping howdies with everyone. Someone must know where she went.

On my way to the docks, I pay a visit to that big cat. As soon as I tap on his cage, he jumps to with a snarl. But he smells the chicken I brought and sits with a huff, licking his lips. I push that chicken through the bars, and he shakes it. Feathers fly as he plucks them off, none too graceful, and swallows the chicken whole.

Finally he looks up, feathers stuck to his mouth and chin, watching me watching him. We're so close, I can smell his chicken-blood breath. He snorts, feathers fluttering from his black lip.

And then—the honest truth—he lies down.

"Ain't you an all-out wonder," I whisper. The big cat cleans his paw with his tongue. "Can't tell what's a-coming next, but I know I don't belong here, in this civilized city. It makes no sense to me. I promise, I'll tell you when I figure it out. I won't leave without saying good-bye."

Just then I hear voices and jump behind the tiger's cage. Them voices sound familiar. I peer around the corner of the cage to get a better look.

There, standing in the lantern glow, are the codfish dandies, Alaire and Alain.

And they ain't alone.

Waddling up to them is that old sausage himself, Hogg Tyler. I see them swap howdies like old friends. Hogg Tyler, who held Gurdy in chains, shot Cam, and even threatened to kill me. At his heels, looking around like a clucking chicken, is that fiddler.

"You!" someone shouts. Both me and the tiger jump to. It's the fiddler—he's pointing at me! On his shout the others turn in my direction, too.

"You wretched hobgoblin!" Hogg Tyler roars, and starts toward me. "I told you we'd see each other again!" Them dandies lower their hats about their faces, trying to hide behind the brims. They dash to a carriage in wait. The tiger roars, running the length of his cage, and I dash, too, away from the green and the streetlamps.

I steal a look over my shoulder, trying to see where they might be. The fiddler's spindly tail is bearing down on me quick. But just then, like a snake hiding in the grass, a new shadow jumps out at me from the alley. He grabs me with fingers sharp as talons. I wince as his hand twists me about and covers my mouth so tight, I can't scream. I can't move, can't even kick my way out of his grip.

He's a small man, but with mightily big shoulders and massive arms.

"Quiet," he whispers rough. "Your life depends upon it."

I still try to twist my way out of his grip, but he's got me good.

I can hear the tiger roaring.

This bull of a man picks me up like a bundle of twigs and slides deeper into the alley. He eases flat against the wall. He don't let go of me as he withdraws his pistol. I try to swallow, but his hold on my throat is tight. I can't find any air. I can barely breathe.

He moves his hand away slowly. He don't have to tell me to stay put when Hogg Tyler's hunting me down. For the first time ever, I listen.

The fiddler walks slow. Hogg Tyer's caught up with him, and they're closing in on us.

"I warned Mother Colby." Hogg heaves. He ain't walking too easy. His boot scrapes against the wooden walkway. "We gots to find this hobgoblin before she warns Annie Christmas!"

"That pip don't know nothing." The fidder glares.

"Mother ain't taking no chances, and if she gets to her afore we do, Annie might figure this out afore we ready. This deal between Mother and Laffite can make us rich."

"I say we quit all this fancy dancing and just do them both in. Now," says the fiddler. "Don't see the sense in keeping some wretched, thieving river rat alive."

"You heard Mother," Hogg Tyler growls. "We don't move on Annie till Laffite gives us the word. We'll kill them all soon enough. Annie Christmas, her sons, that hobgoblin pip. Then I'll have my revenge for her da killing me brother."

The fiddler spits into the dark. His spit lands close to us. But this bullish man, he don't flinch. "That pip ain't natural, all that red hair."

Hogg Tyler grunts. "Don't be so addled. She ain't just any thieving river rat. You just angry because she plays the fiddle better than you. My dog plays the fiddle better than you. You aim to shoot my dog?"

They're near atop of us. This bullish man pushes me deeper

into the alley, following the wall. The fiddler veers sharp and takes a slow, careful step toward the alley. He's peering in the shadows, coming our way.

"What's Mother going to do about the Laffites, then?" the fiddler whispers.

"She's got a plan. Don't you worry none," Hogg Tyler growls. "She's about had it with that dandified pirate acting so high and mighty while we do all his dirty work. He ain't no better than the rest of us."

That fiddler peers into the alley's dark—right at us. If he takes another step, he'll see us for sure.

This ox don't wait. In the same tick of time, he drops me and shoots his pistol. The fiddler stumbles backward in surprise, clutching his chest. Before he falls, the fiddler whines, "There!"

Then the ox spins me about and hisses, "Run!"

But he don't let go of me. His grip on my shoulder tightens, right down to the bone. He pushes me along. He veers sharp, ducking behind a door, shoving me close against a wall. A moment later Hogg Tyler and another man run past us, yelling for the others to follow. Only when them weasels disappear down the street does this ox release me.

"My brother sent me to find you." He spits out the words while dragging me along like a sack of rice. "Looks like I found more than what he wanted. My brother will be disappointed."

"Brother?" This man don't look like much. His clothes ain't the fancified shirts with lace cuffs, but a plain shirt with wide blue sleeves, a bandana wrapped about his head. He's wearing two pistols, and a saber hangs from his hip. He's a rough-and-tumble, about as bloody as they come, and not some civilized codfish.

"Dominique You," he growls, giving me a good shake. "And my brother Jean Laffite won't be pleased, not one lick, with any of this."

Chapter Twenty-Six

This man Dominique You returns me to the pirate patroon. And as Jean Laffite lays eyes on me he wears a telling scowl, as deep as the ocean just beyond.

"I'm glad to see you survived your adventure." He taps his cane. "But you'll excuse us, *petite protégée*. You need your rest."

"I ain't tired."

But the patroon raises his cane and points to my room. He aims to use that cane if I don't move, so I oblige. As I slog toward the stairs he and Dominique step into the parlor, shutting the door behind them.

I may be moving, but I ain't going to any room. Instead, I ease atop the stairs. I sit real still and close my eyes so I can listen better.

"It seems Mother Colby plans to doublecross you and take over the river routes for herself," growls the bulldog Dominique You. "Make herself queen of the river?"

"She plans to overthrow us, does she?" I hear Jean Laffite pacing across the room, tapping his cane with every step.

"Just as planned, Mother Colby is after Annie and her sons, but Annie won't go down without a fight. All this because you chase rumors that Annie Christmas and Dan Fillian know about Blackbeard's treasure?"

"Do I look like a stupid man, Dominique? That treasure is just a fairy tale. It's the Mississippi herself, there's the real treasure. Fillian controlled the trade routes with an iron fist. The king had his secrets: what routes to take to avoid authorities, which authorities he could sway, schedules of delivery, hidden caches. That's how we move around this embargo. Surely he passed the information on to his pip. That river rat is valuable, more so than any story-time treasure. Now, as I see it if Mother Colby and her scum are after Annie, that's good for us. No matter who wins in that battle, it's one less claim to the throne. I, for one, won't get in the way. It's a tragedy, oui, but we must make sure that we are in position to inherit the crown."

This talk turns my blood cold. Them very men who shook their hands in a deal with Annie are out to get her and her boyos. Ain't nothing worse than a man who goes back on his word. I clench my teeth and make a fist.

"Aren't you afraid?' someone whispers behind me. I jump near out of my drawers. I ain't heard Catiche slip up on me. "Oncle says that Colby woman is a real scoundrel, a murderer, and a thief."

"Ain't seen nothing *but* liars, murderers, and thieves in this city," I whisper.

"No, Oncle protects you now." She wags her head. "It's a strange life, yours. You play with rats, and murderers hunt you down. Who protects you now, if it's not Oncle?"

"Da taught me, you learn to protect yourself." I turn back to the parlor. I can't hear their voices anymore. But now I know the truth of it: the Laffites keep me here because they think I know about Da's business. Mother Colby and that Hogg Tyler are after Annie and Gurdy to take over the river. I turn to face Catiche, eye to eye. "I ain't used to saying please. I ain't proper, as you let me know well enough. You don't want me here any more than I want to stay. It suits us both for me to go."

"You make no sense. Oncle gives you all that you need. He protects you," Catiche whispers, confused. I hope my da is alive. I don't know if he is. But Gurdy is alive.

I shake my head slow. "That pirate's going after the only family I have left. Gurdy and Annie are heading into a trap. It's a bloody damn business, and I'm in the middle of it. Besides, I belong on the big river. It took me a while to figure that out, for all the sorrow she done me. But I ain't living under the heels of no one, not even your uncle. Now I just want to go home."

Catiche sits silent, her thoughts spinning like an eddy.

I keep talking, hoping she hears the full measure of my words. "Some are hunting Gurdy because of me. I have to warn him. If you knew your sister was in danger, wouldn't you go to her?"

It seems a slow, long moment before she looks to me. I can't tell if she's smiling or scowling. Says she, "If Marie was in trouble, no one could keep me from helping her. And surely my life would be easier without you under my feet. So oui, I'll help you."

And we sit in our own parley. She tells me her plan, and I'm beginning to think maybe there's more to her than frocks and frippery. Then I go back to my room and wait for her signal. I tighten the strap holding the spy case against my back. This will take you there, Da said.

I ain't wearing a dress. Not ever again. I got the front of my shift tucked up in my sash. I got my boots. That's enough to get me where I'm going. Catiche comes in with a sack of peaches and bread. She brought a rope, which I wind up tight. I got a knife, too. It ain't a Big Sally, but in a pinch it'll do.

But that ain't all I've got with me. Sure enough, I'm taking that fancified fiddle. It was a gift, after all, and don't I know it's impolite to refuse a gift.

I am uncivilized, true enough. But I ain't impolite.

Chapter Twenty-Seven

All day I wait in my room. I don't even come out for supper. Then the sun goes down, and I keep waiting. Can't tell what time it is. But it's time enough for everyone to retreat to their rooms. The house goes into a deep sleep. Not even Sarah rummages around with her late night chores. It's so quiet, I can hear the boats on the river ring the all's well. The only ones moving about the yard are the pirate's guards.

And then in the moment of all this quiet, Catiche shrieks. Suddenly, the house erupts like a fountain of water. I hear boots scrambling up the stairs, men shouting, and Marie wailing about some terror. I hear the three pips wailing, too. Catiche is screaming wild.

Now I jump to, and in three leaps I reach the window. Like a spider, I climb onto the roof and make my careful way to the balcony. I take the rope, loop the end around the iron, tie it with a bowline, and slide down. She's still screaming bloody murder. The windows are all alit. I can see shadows run across the shades.

And the guards leave their post. Now, it's my turn.

My palms burn as I slide down the rope, but the burning ain't slowing me down. I jump the last bit to the ground. And then I run like my tail's on fire.

Chapter Twenty-Eight

Staying to the side of the ditches, I keep to the planks, out of the mud. My every step bounces the wood: it's like running on a long deck. It won't take them but a moment to figure out I'm missing, so I got to cover as much distance as I can.

All too soon the devil's on my heels. I hear men shout. Someone's clanging a bell in warning, waking all within earshot.

People are starting to wake up and join the boodle gathering in the street. I hear horses hurtling toward me and the pirate patroon boom, "To the river! The river! Find that girl!"

Catiche did what she could to give me some time. But I put my own plan into play. Stealing another look over my shoulder, I see their torchlights gathering. I turn into an alley, making my way to the green.

Da told me once, there's a reason why civilized folk call us rats. A rat is special good at sneaking in the shadows and scrambling through tight places. But most of all, rats—particularly scrawny ones like me—are special good at stealing.

The circus wrangler keeps his ring of keys hanging just inside his wagon door. He snores, a long, slow wind. I have to be quick if I'm going to make this work. The wrangler must not hear the ruckus outside, for he keeps snoring as I creep up—then I smell the drink. He's in a corned stupor, so steep, he don't move as I pinch his keys.

I dash off to the animal cages. Just that fast, tick tick tick, I shuffle through the keys and find the one that matches each padlock. I let loose the parrots first. They erupt out of the cage in a fountain of feathers.

I let loose the doves, and the peacocks, and the roosters, all wild in their newfound freedom, crowing and cooing and calling out in screechy confusion.

I let loose the dogs, who chase the birds. Their wild barking spurs them into a frenzy. Then them dogs chase each other in circles, all snarls and growls.

I let loose the toothless puma, the geese and the pigs, the donkey and the bear cub, too. Soon the green is one confused eddy, a whirling of noise and bodies.

Just then the greasy wrangler comes out screaming. He's stumbling about, not fully awake, and powerful vexed at his carnival of animals stampeding around him. He snaps a whip, trying to get them back in their cages, then shoots a pistol, hoping to scare them down. But that doesn't slow me none.

The last cage I come to is the tiger's cage. For another tick in time, we stare eye to eye.

"They'll likely shoot you outright or chop off your legs to keep you from running. But you deserve a chance to be free."

"There she is!" someone shouts behind me.

It's the pirates, shooting and fighting in the stampede of carnival animals. Dogs trained to attack anything that moves now attack them men. The men's shouts turn into shrieks of terror.

Feathers are flying thick as fog. Two men who came too close to the bucking donkey fall like flapjacks, groaning in pain. The wrangler, more teched than ever, snaps his whip at man and animal alike. He squirrels around, fighting those shooting at his stock.

Quick as his whip, I unbolt the tiger's cage, and then I run fast, like a keel with its sail up. And that tiger, he's running at my heels. He ain't chasing me, ain't hunting me; he's running with me, and we're heading straight to the big river.

The docks are a-flurry with confusion. Sailors and keelers

and families of flatters gather, all in a wonder at what spectacle is bearing down upon them. Ain't they surprised to see me a-coming, running fast as the wind!

But their surprise turns to fear on seeing the tiger at my heels, and they flutter like chickens scattering to hide. Some rush back up the levee and right into Laffite's men. I weave past all of them. They can't hold me down, can't hold me back! Not ever again!

I jump from one boat to the next, looking for an empty deck. The boats are moored so close, it's like jumping stones across a creek.

I veer sharp onto the empty deck of a keeler. Suddenly, a man bursts out of the cabin, readying his musket. He shouts his surprise to see me hopping across his deck, and near falls back on himself when he sees the tiger. He trips overboard to escape.

But there, tied to this keeler, a skiff rocks gentle in the river's current. And just beyond is the big river herself.

Quick, I jump into the skiff, easing to its center. I look up to see the tiger standing still now, looking out across the river.

"You followed me this far," I tell that tiger. "You looking to go elsewhere now?"

On the docks Laffite's men are fighting their way through the onrush of people.

"You got to decide, Tiger. Them men have their temper up, and they're coming for me. They aim to take us both back to them cages. They aim to keep us under their heels."

I look to Tiger. Don't know if he's really thinking about what'll happen next if he follows this river rat into the wilds of the Mississip.

But in the next moment he jumps into the skiff.

The boat rocks as he lands. The big cat dances wobbly, his tail whirling behind him as he finds his balance. And then he settles in with a yawn. I gather the oars and begin to row away from the dock.

"Let's go find Annie Christmas."

Part Three

July
1812

Everyone belongs somewhere, like birds knowing the sky be their home. Them birds that don't fly, they dream of flyin', says Da.

Living on the river ain't an easy life, not for the weak-bodied or the weak-hearted. But for those of us who be her sons and daughters, ain't no other place we call home.

I'm right behind you always.

Some others are chasing our tail now. Them pirates Laffite and that murderous Mother Colby and her brigade, they're all hunting us down.

But after all this while after that happened, I'm finally headin' home, back to that big river.

Chapter Twenty-Nine

It's some days afore I finally escape the city stink and reach the wide Mississip. I breathe deep the familiar smell of them piney woods, swampy grasslands, and fish; of wet moss and mud, and the muskiness of the very earth itself. That big river's changed, true enough. Sandbanks have shifted, and old landmarks have disappeared. Whole islands and whole towns, all gone. But for all that change, it still smells the same.

Sweeter than honey, says Da.

It's the honest truth, Tiger's stayed with me. That first day he was a shadow, nothing more than flashes of orange and white flickering through the underbrush. But he kept close and by the end of that day, he walked neck to neck with me with a soft *brrr*, like he was saying, "Ain't this happifying?"

Freetown, that's where we're going. It has a reputation for meanery and shecoonery, but that ain't ever stopped Da. It ain't ever stopped Annie. "Freetown ain't a real town," I say to Tiger. We've ditched the skiff, and now we're moving quickly through the tangle. Tiger trots, his tail sways loose, easy as a slow-moving current. "We stopped there every time we made a trip this way. It's a hidey-hole for river rats. That's where we'll find Annie Christmas."

We spend a night by a fishing hole, and come daybreak, I lie on the grasses, taking in everything around me. Where the water pools, cypress grow, moss hanging heavy on their branches like some beards on old men. Skeeters hum, but that ain't the only river music I hear. Frogs are all a-chuckle. The kingbirds sing *zeeerr*, and the swamp sparrows trill. And flying above it all, a whistling osprey chirps on the wind. For all the sorrow that river had done them, too, it's a wonder that life come back.

I keep looking over my shoulder for them mannies belonging to the pirates Laffite, or a rogue belonging to Mother Colby, or even the circus wrangler looking for his big cat. I know they're coming for us.

"Don't you worry none," I say to Tiger. "Da taught me good."

Them that's chasing us, they can chase us to the end of the world, but they ain't going to find us. Who-op! River born, that's me.

Suddenly, Tiger crouches low. He stalks a toad—a big one, king of the pond. Just as Tiger pounces, the toadie bounces. He ain't king for nothing. Tiger follows him into the pond, as much river rat as he is cat. He splashes mightily, chasing down that king toadie. But the king is king for a reason. He mocks that big cat with a loud, throaty croak as he slips away in the swirling mud and out of reach.

Tiger stands, watching the water settle, the king long gone.

But it turns out something else is hunting King Toadie. It ain't appreciating some big cat taking over. It rumbles in the shadows, and the water boils around a log.

Just then the log moves. It slices through the water. It's a gator, true enough, and from the looks of him, this here is Big Boss Gator himself.

And he's a-going after Tiger!

"Tiger!" I jump to, hard as I might to make the earth tremble. But all that happens is the dust puffs about my boots. I can see the gator's eyes float like two white balls across the surface. And then he sinks.

"Tiger!" I throw the biggest rounders I can find. I aim for them eyes. Big Boss splashes and snaps them jaws. But Tiger already sees Big Boss a-coming. He bounces like a rabbit out of the water. Big Boss disappears and is gone.

Tiger ain't the only one with a powerful need to eat.

Fishing is best in the early morn. But I ain't willing to share my fishing hole with any gator, so I look for a creek. I fish the way Gurdy showed me: Stand very still with the patience of a stone, and don't twitch a toe or even blink. Look deep to see through the ripple, and when a fish comes too close, maybe lingering about your feet, hold to until it thinks it safe. Then quick, quick! Scoop it with both hands and throw it to the shore. Scoop, don't grab—that's the secret. Once it's ashore, use the knife. Don't make it suffer. It had a good life, and now it has purpose, says Gurdy.

Before I have a chance to cook my fish proper, Tiger takes it and swallows it whole. Then, he sits on the bank and waits for another.

This time I scoop a real beaut with black stripes running down its silvery, shiny body.

"A striper! Looks just like you!"

Tiger snorts. The striper ain't giving up easy. It hits the ground hard and flops around like one of Da's flapjacks, slapping Tiger's whiskers. The big cat snorts and shakes his head. He sniffs the fish, and the striper bounces away. Then Tiger pounces, and the fish is done for.

I stand rock still, waiting for the next one. This one here is mine! I see a flicker of silver dart from behind a rock, and stiffen every muscle. Come a little closer, fish, closer . . .

Suddenly, Tiger roars as he splashes through the creek. He jumps so far, water splashes like rain falling upside down. He jumps with such force, I fall on my backside, and the fish skitters away.

I missed my breakfast, but I don't mind. I ain't ever seen a cat love water as much as Tiger. Every stream, every pond, every watering hole we pass, Tiger splashes in it, sometimes with a roar. And sometimes I join him. Who-op!

As he plays in the shallows I think, Ain't he some. His ribs don't show as much. His fur ain't so ragged. Every day passing, he seems to grow more into them big paws.

And so it goes, day in, day out. Night comes early. We follow a river of moonbeams deeper into the marsh, where I catch me a fish of my own. Using cypress moss, I light a fire, and its embers spark like falling stars. I lay my boots out close to the flames, drying them out, and turn the fish on the stick. Tiger jumps to, standing still as stone.

Just then there's a long jagged sound that tears through the air—a puma's hunting. Tiger roars back, a ripsnorting roar that puts that mousy cat to shame. The puma quiets now. Tiger's taking it all in, true enough, his ears and tail a-twitching. Then his mouth curves, like he's smiling.

Don't know what moves me, but I hold my hand out, fingers a-tremble, and I touch his fur. Tiger watches as my fingertips dance across his black stripes. He's softer than horsehair, softer than dog hair. His fur twitches under my touch. Then he snorts and lies down. He rolls on his back, paws to the air.

As crooked as that Mississip flows, it ain't near as crooked as this swampy way. We're deep in the tangle now. We're far off the Natchez, moving through dangerous land filled with all sorts of varmints. Since I can't see the river, I climb into the trees, high as I might. The stars let me know where I am. And below, Tiger roars like he's singing to them stars. That's some day we had, he's saying.

Chapter Thirty

Freetown is still a ways away. Come morning light, I'm stomping to move, but Tiger's slow. It's starting to vex me. I'm in a worm of worry over Gurdy.

"We ain't got time for all this twaddle! Get your wiggle on, Tiger! We need to move out!" And he does; just like that, he shoots off into the tangle. In the wrong direction.

That big cat don't seem to have his mind set on anything but chasing his fancy. If it ain't frogs and birds, it's squirrels and ducks and coons.

"Ain't you some catawampus friend!" I shout, my dander fully up. "This ain't the time for playful whims!"

But hell and damnation, that Tiger disappears into the tangle, his roar more like chuckles.

Well, I ain't waiting. Not for some chucklehead. I tighten the spy case against my back, hang that fancy fiddle from the strap, and take off in my own direction. I aim to find Annie Christmas and warn Gurdy about the storm coming and the bounty on all our heads.

Tiger roars back, and something squeals.

"I ain't waiting for you! I ain't!" I shout back. Da was right about cats. This one's more trouble than a snake with its tail twisted.

Then suddenly, Tiger's roar turns into a wail, a bawling that's enough to stop me in my tracks. Something's wrong.

"Tiger?" I swallow my wrathy just that fast, and I run straight to that roar. And there I find Tiger hanging by his hind leg between twin oaks. Some fool hunter had forgotten his snare.

Tiger twists in fury, trying to grab the cord with his front claws, but he can't reach it. He wails all the more, his leg bleeding where the cord cuts the skin.

"Tiger!" I run close as I dare to the big cat. In his pain he swipes at me. I duck it easy enough, like some fancy dance. Easing round the trunk, I look for the end of the rope.

"Tiger, Tiger," I whisper, like singing a lullaby. He ain't so wrathy now, but he's still mightily pitiable. He whines, watching me as I bring out my knife. The trapper had thrown the rope over the lowest hanging branch. There's no telling how long the trap's been set. It ain't such a good trap, for the animals in this forest have avoided it easy enough. But Tiger's still learning the ways of this world.

The knife is dull, and cutting the rope is more like sawing through wood. It cuts through one strand, and then another. Tiger whines, watching me.

"It's a hard lesson, learning to do what you're told." I saw my way through another strand. Tiger twists, breaking the last strand, and falls free of the snare. I pull the loop off his leg while he lies there licking his paw.

"Well, it looks like you need to stay off that paw for a bit. Guess we ain't going nowhere this day." I take some water and clean the fur. "It ain't so bad."

Tiger brushes his head against me, purring softly.

"No need to say you're sorry." I pluck his ears. "Can't hardly blame you for going off on your own. I've been accused of that crime myself. Besides, you and I, we're all we've got. Ain't right for me to walk out on you, especially since this ain't your place. It won't happen again. Don't you worry none. I'm good at keeping my word."

Chapter Thirty-One

Something's hunting.

Tiger's ears perk up and forward. Suddenly, he jumps to, at the ready. He's a-growling, full of menace. He ain't fooling. It's only been a day since his trapping, but he don't even pay a never-mind about his leg hurting.

Something heard his roaring and comes to check it out. Something big enough to put the frights in him.

It walks too heavy to be a bear. And too loud to be a hunter. And it stinks to high heaven. I know that smell. Tiger's got it right to be this afeared. It's enough to get mine going. I kick dirt on the fire and strap on my case.

Tiger's ears flatten. His lips curl back, his fangs showing. He hisses hard and sharp. I ain't ever seen Tiger so cracked. He's raging as the big river herself.

I step back slowly, my own hackles tingling.

It's a big wild boar thundering our way. Da and me hunted enough wild boar to know its best to make ourselves scarce.

Then I hear something else, too. Barking. It's a boodle of dogs chasing that hog, and they're a-coming toward us.

"Get your wiggle on, Tiger! Where there's a dog, there's a pirate or a swamper. And where's there's men, there's guns!"

The barking gets louder. I know I can't outrun them, but I can surely hide.

Tiger can run if he has a mind to, and I expect he will. But he stays—he don't run away on me! It turns out there's a peculiar similarity between tigers and river rats. We both climb trees. And the tupelo offers some safety. In two heaves Tiger finds a branch to settle on. I take a bit longer and climb a bit higher. I settle on my own branch, not far from him.

There in the tree, we wait.

Soon enough, the giant boar charges through the clearing. That swampy monster is bigger than Tiger, chomping his tusks and ready to rip a man apart. He veers sharp, disappearing into the reeds. Not long after, the dogs—there's three of them—come.

They sniff the cooled fire and bones of the fish. They sniff around the tree, around the swamp. They stay to the shallows, sniffing the thicket. They start a-howling something fierce.

Four rogues come up, hollering as loud as the dogs.

"Git 'em, boyos! Git 'em!"

The dogs charge through the clearing, the men at their tails. I near pity them if they catch up to that boar. It'll be some bloody rough-and-tumble.

It takes a long while for my hackles to ease. I expect the same is true for Tiger.

We stay put long past the sunset. We're so high in them trees, I can see stars light up the treetops. The river sparkles, a flickering ribbon trailing into the distance. As a gentle breeze dulls the heat I feel like I'm in a lullaby, sitting high on top of the world.

Chapter Thirty-Two

There's a dozen chickens clucking, pacing inside their rickety coop.

Tiger crouches, creeping through the brush. He's eyeing them chickens, and he aims to get one.

He ain't the only one. I'm looking to get my share, too.

It's just a shanty, the sorriest-looking place in the world. There's smoke roiling out of the chimney. Splintered and cracked logs have mud stuffed into spaces. The roof, what's left of it, is made of rough shakes. The garden's gone wild like them woods.

"Hold steady," I whisper.

But Tiger ain't listening. He explodes from the bush, an orange streak of lightning jumping over the coop's fence, and pounces on them chickens. With a roar he catches one in his claws. Others scream in every direction, flying right out of the coop.

A man bursts from the door flap, a pistol in his hand.

"Who goes there?" he shouts, fierce and ready.

Tiger twists about, ears flat, crouching low to the ground, chicken in mouth.

The man shrills, "What the devil are you?"

I burst from behind the shanty. I'm a-screaming like the river banshee at the end of days. It's just a tick in time, but it's all I need. Racing right up to the man like a bull, I hit him square. He stumbles, too stunned to catch himself, and falls onto his backside with a big wallop. The wallop sets off the pistol and sends him rolling.

Tiger scrambles now, chicken in mouth, disappearing back to the bushes.

I ain't so lucky, as the man catches me but good.

"What's this?" Behind me someone chuckles. He must of come off the water, hearing Tiger's charge. Even before I turn about, someone gets me by the shoulder and hauls me to the shanty. "Lookee! Lookee! I catch me a wee mouse!"

It's the ragged group hunting the hog. Looks like me and Tiger have stumbled onto their hidey-hole! The rail-skinny man rises to his feet as two others come out of the shanty.

"I know that whelp!" says one big man. "That's Fillian's girl. I thought Laffite had hold on her?"

"Heard tell she got away from the Laffites." The first one shakes me. "I dee-clare, we hit the mother lode with this one! Mother might pay us real handsome for finding this lost little mouse. Or Laffite might even pay a fine ransom to get her back."

"Hold on," another man says, pulling out his pistol. He's gone white as a sheet, looking to them woods. "That thing that got our chickens. She's with some devil cat."

"You best let me go!" I screech, atrembling in fear. It ain't real trembles. These rogues only got one oar in the water. Let them think me a cowering mouse. I raise my voice loud so that Tiger will hear me. "P-P-Please, I'm a-begging you! It's the devil cat himself! That Mississip Lion—he's after me! And he'll kill you, it's true!"

And then Tiger roars. Didn't expect him to get here so fast. It's hard swallowing my smile. I hide it by getting my spunk on.

"You must be new to these parts, or else you'd know," I wail woefully. "There are swampy monsters here! And this one's rare as gold, but much, much more dangerous. He's got fangs a foot long and claws sharp enough to scratch the skin off a gator! He's powerful hungry, and he has my scent. Now he's got yours, too! Run!"

Tiger roars again. Them men, they're as jittery as corn over a fire.

"Ain't ever seen nothing like that afore," says the rail-skinny man holding me. He's trembling so, his knees are knocking. "It's the Mississip Lion, for sure!"

The four of them stumble back, seeing a flash of orange through the underbrush. One man screams. Another pulls out a pistol.

Finally Tiger bursts through the brush, and the men shriek, scrambling like chickens. The two of us—Tiger roaring and me screaming—dash back through the underbrush. I ain't worried about them following us: they're still screaming in the other direction.

We don't stop running, all the way back to the tree. Quick I fetch the spy case and the fiddle, and we keep running.

Now I know what they know. The bounty on Annie and her boyos are bringing every manner of viper on our tails.

Chapter Thirty-Three

⚓

Freetown ain't a full-grown town. It ain't more than a few ramshackle buildings set deep in the woods. It don't look like much, but Da says it's a mighty important place in the scheme of things.

Tiger sniffs the air, his tail snaking behind him. I lay my hand on his head as he bumps against my knee.

We keep walking, looking for any signs of Annie and her boyos. The buildings are a heap of twigs scarred with fire. It reeks of death. It's as if the earth ripped itself open. And in the ripping, it let loose a spew of fire and rage. Bodies of men and animals lie scattered around the streets, picked by scavengers and shrouded in clouds of flies.

There's some belly left to an ox that had died in the street. A vulture is perched atop the ox's rump, pulling entrails out of the ox's backside. With a grunt Tiger approaches the carcass and begins sniffing. The vulture squawks and flaps its wings as the big cat gets close. But Tiger stands his ground.

"Tiger, we ain't got time for this twaddle!" I tell him. "Leave the bird alone to its meal."

Tiger snarls as he sticks his nose into the exploding belly. Suddenly, he yowls hard and low, as if something chomps his nose. He jumps backward as a coon explodes out of the ox, its bushy tail full out. Its nose soaked in blood, the banded coon stands at its full height and hisses at Tiger.

Tiger returns the hiss, batting the coon, but that coon won't be bullied and jumps forward. Tiger rises on his hind legs as he roars. I'm thinking he's going to pounce, and I bet that coon thinks it, too. Quickly the coon puffs itself up all the more and shrieks almighty. Tiger yelps in surprise.

"He's got you beat!" I laugh. "You big striped bunny rabbit!"

Tiger yowls again, falling backward as that coon jumps forward again. I let loose such a belly-rolling laugh, I double over.

Suddenly, shot rings out, the ball screaming close to my ear. My laugh rolls into screams as Tiger falls back, blood oozing down his leg.

"Tiger!" I screech like the end of days.

Another shot is fired. I swerve to see who's firing. I spin so hard, I trip on my own feet, and fall. The spy case cracks me in the ribs.

"Don't shoot!" I wave my hands, gathering my legs beneath me. "Don't shoot!

Chapter Thirty-Four

⚓

"I'm sorry! I'm sorry!" Cane shakes his head. "I thought that big cat was attacking you!"

As Annie's boyos step out of the woods my innards swirl like a leaf lost on some wild wind. I found them at last.

"If it helps"—Cully steps up, wearing a sly grin and holding his pistol out to me—"you can use my pistol to shoot Cane. Eye for an eye, and all that!"

"Shoot him in the leg," Cam shouts from behind. "Fair is fair!"

"Hold off on that!" Cane shouts, fully afeared I might just shoot him.

Then Gurdy steps out, and that old anger rises in me. I tighten my fist.

"There be no more shooting here, little River." Gurdy kneels next to me, big tears rolling down his beard.

"You *left* me!" I hiss so hard, I spit. "That's not what kin do, no matter what!"

Gurdy smiles and holds me close. "You right. That not what kin do."

I take a breath, and slowly my anger eases. "Can you fix Tiger?"

He speaks in his own language, the one his father taught him. He eases closer, slow as a snail, to the big cat.

I ease to the ground, holding Tiger's head in my lap and stroking his neck. He's breathing in rasps and moaning. Tiger lies there, heaving and growling. He's bleeding like a river where the bullet clawed his leg.

"No worry none, little River," says Gurdy as he examines the wound. "It not so bad. The bullet done strike no bone. Cover his eyes and stroke him. Let him know he safe."

He strokes the big cat, too. He tells Cully what to look for in plants, and Cully runs to find the flowers. Cody and his twin moon, Cay, follow. The other boyos, Chance, Coffee, and Crow, stand guard around us. Gurdy, too, gathers other plants, taking some mud. He kneads the mix together like it was bread. He places the kneaded poultice on Tiger's leg.

Finally Annie Christmas comes up and kneels behind us. Tiger growls, so she keeps her distance.

"Girl, I thought you safe with Laffite. What possessed you to come into these river wilds by your lonesome?" She tries reaching out to me, but I recoil. "I ain't left you, River. My own Cully wrote the note and delivered it to you in person. He come back, telling me you wouldn't even see him. Laffite told him you decided to stay. He said you were safe enough with him, and for me not to worry!"

"I got no such note." I growl just like Tiger. "I ain't even seen Cully. That Laffite said you told me to stay put."

"You never were one to stay put when you were told." Cully chuckles as he hands Gurdy the gathered flowers and roots. I shoot him a prickly look. He swallows, losing his smile and kneeling. "We thought you safe, River. And we believed Laffite when he said it was you who decided to stay behind. It wasn't until we heard tell about some orange-headed hobgoblin and a big orange cat roaming these woods that we thought maybe something's gone a-wiggle here. We come to Freetown looking for you. Ma wouldn't let us do nothing else till she knew you were safe."

"I weren't safe in that fancy city. There's more sharks roaming in those harbors than in the ocean."

"We didn't know, River." Cully smiles gentlelike. "But you're safe now, and all's well."

"Except Cane shot Tiger!" Tiger moans, slapping his tail.

"My offer's still open." Cully grins, patting his pistol.

"I should have known that bilge rat would try something like this," Annie cuts in. "Damn it to hell! He aims to take over the river himself."

"That's why I come to warn Gurdy—and you."

Laffite. Mother Colby. Hogg Tyler. Even them twin dandies Alain and Alaire. It's like some powerful eddy swirling around me, its undertow trying its best to drag me under. I ain't going to let that happen.

"You ain't telling me to stay put, not ever again," I say to Annie Christmas. "You ain't leaving me off, not with any fancy pants, not ever again."

"You are right in that." Annie gives me a hug. "That's not what kin do."

And that eddy inside me calms, and I let her hug me.

Gurdy smears the kneaded mud, leaf, and flower poultice on Tiger's haunches. Coby leans in close to hand him a stick with spiderwebs wrapped around it. Gurdy unwraps the webby net and places it over Tiger's wound. "He will hunt again."

Tiger *brrrs*. . . . He closes his lids in a drowsy sleep.

Cully smiles at me. "Trouble seems to follow you like some bad friend."

"So, tell me what that old weasel did," Annie says.

I tell Annie all I seen in the city. I tell her about Madame Rochon knowing Annie. Tell her about them dandified twins in a handshake of a deal with Hogg Tyler and Mother Colby. And I tell her about the bounty Mother Colby put on Annie's head and on her sons'. Prolly on my head, too. Then I tell her about Laffite's own words—that it would be one less claim to the throne if Annie was done in, and he intended to take advantage of the situation.

Annie's fingers tap on her musket.

"Expected as much from that rabble Mother Colby. But Laffite, well, I was hoping for a bit more truth-saying. Ain't it the way of it. Ah, little River, your da left us too soon."

"Wonder what bounty is on my head." Cully hoots. "I'm worth twice as much as Cam. Certainly more than Chance. I'm prettier!"

Chance kicks dirt, keen on the woods, his musket readied. "I say it's high time we get out of here. Those hunters after River are prolly well close now."

Annie seems particularly tetchy. "Well, we ain't going nowhere tonight. Coffee and Cay, set the perimeter. Let's build a fire here. Cody and Cam, you take to the river and fish us some supper."

I wince, feeling pain in my ribs. Moving the spy case, I hear the glass within rattle. I wince again.

"Da would beat me good to see it broke," I say.

Annie smiles tender, easing next to me. She raises the shift. "You bruised your ribs all right, but it's nothing a good night's rest won't take care of. Your tiger friend may take a couple more days, but we ain't got more time to give him."

She takes the lenses out of the spyglass and whistles as she looks it over. "The glass is still good. The handle is cracked, but the case is strong. That's some old wood your da used to make this. And look at them fancified carvings! Crow can fix this easy."

She pulls apart the two sections.

"What's this?" She whistles as she peers at the carvings on the spyglass handle. I ain't paid particular attention to those before. They seem like a boodle of dots. But then Annie starts twisting the handle. "River? Did you know about this?"

I look closer, trying to make out what's she's talking about. Taking the glass, I turn the handle slowly, fingering the dots. I smile, seeing these dots line up in a familiar pattern. Da taught me how to read my way around the river, and it's like I'm reading the river again. I recognize the big dot—the island with the blockhouse. I recognize the bend of the river and old shores we used to pass. Fingering the dots more, I follow another line that moves off the river, and I know it as one of our trade routes, and more dots as more towns and other stands following the inland road. There's more dots sprayed out across the carving, but I don't recognize them. At the edge of them dots, Da had carved a fancified *R*. R for River. Da had carved my letter the day he gave me the spyglass. Take good care of it, he said. And it'll take you where you need to go.

"These dots here." I show Annie. "They're the river before

the quake. These dots moving off the river show one of Da's favorite trade routes. But these others falling off the edge, I can't tell what they are or where they go."

"Hell bells, little River!" Annie whistles something fierce. "Do you know what you have here? Them dots are the Devil's Backbone. It's as wild as wild gets."

"That's where I saw Little Harpe," says Crow, coming over with Cully. "That's one dangerous swamp, Mam. And that old Harpe is as crazy as a bucket of frogs."

As I roll the handle again, the top twists off and two coins fall out, one silver and one gold. Crow and Cully whoop at the sight of them, and the other boyos rush over.

"The Devil's Backbone?" I roll the coins over. "Why would Da make a map of that place? That last night at the blockhouse, you and Da and Annie were talking about how Mason found Blackbeard's treasure. He was smiling one of his hidey smiles and telling Annie, there's always a treasure map. Is that what this is, a treasure map?"

"That old snapping turtle." Annie shakes her head, smiling. "I remember that smile. Well, hell's bells, little River. Your da knew about the treasure all along!"

"Well, keep your drawers on, Mam," Crow says, looking at the map on the case. "This here map ain't complete. It might say where to go, but it don't say nothing 'bout where it's hid."

"Da told me," I say. "He told me at the blockhouse to keep this glass safe because it'll take me there. That's what he said."

"Take you where?" Annie eyes the coins closely.

I shake my head, fighting for the memory. "You were talking about Blackbeard's treasure and Mason finding it . . . and Little Harpe stealing it from Mason. That's it! He told me to find Harpe! Bet Harpe knows where the treasure is."

Cully whistles, and his brothers start jigging about. "It's real, Ma—Blackbeard's gold!"

"Come tomorrow, we set off to find Little Harpe," says Annie. "We're going after that treasure."

Chapter Thirty-Five

The next morning the *Big River's Daughter* rocks gentle on the current. I smile at the sight of her shiny self. She's got a new cabin, and a new prow, and a new shiny deck. Don't I feel glorious now, like when my da sang some familiar song to me at twilight on the Mississip.

Tiger grunts and sits. He ain't impressed.

"Get your wiggle on, Tiger." I scratch his ear. He follows at my heels, his tail hanging loose and swaying easy. Then he snorts, lifting his muzzle up as if to call me back down the plank.

"Ain't no worries," I say, bouncing across to the boat. "Come along, big cat!"

On deck Cully and Cam hoot. Cody and Coby, too. Tiger eyes them and spits. He only tolerates these others, and they only tolerate him, too. I expect it an uneasy truce.

Crow shakes his head. "Ain't no one told you, cats don't belong on boats?"

"Women and children don't belong on them boats neither, so say you men," I shout back. "That ain't stopped us yet."

Annie blows her smoke rings. She and Gurdy stand on the prow, waiting.

Finally Gurdy comes across the plank. He kneels close to Tiger, and he says, "Come, friend."

There you are, and there you ain't. Tiger snorts and gets up. That big cat still limps, but he follows Gurdy across the plank. And as Tiger reaches the deck them boyos move aside like parting waters to let him pass. Tiger harrumphs, moving to the aft deck, and stretches full out.

"Welcome aboard." I smile, scratching his chin.

Now them boyos ashore move quick to untie the mooring, then race up the plank before others pull it up. The *Big River's Daughter* begins to drift. Annie takes the big oar on the stern and steers into the current.

"My loves," says she, "let's get to it, now! We got us a treasure to find!"

Don't you know it, them boyos push and pull at the oars. As the keeler slices through the water Cam starts to sing. I take my place atop the cabin and pull out that fancy fiddle. I start a fast rowing melody.

Some rows up, but we rows down,
All the way to Shawneetown.
Pull away, pull away.

Tiger roars, his tail tap-tapping, but it's more like he's singing. And we roll merrily along!

It's some days before my ribs don't ache so much, and Tiger don't limp so much, when we reach the tavern. The tavern's set way back in the woods. Ain't nothing more than a small lean-to that looks any moment to fall in on itself. There's a big chimney, and black smoke coils out of it like some swampy snake. Ain't no windows, so I can't see in. But more important is that they can't see out.

I stand just outside the entrance in the shadows with Tiger behind me. He ain't liking this one bit. He's looking wary, his ears twitching about.

I look inside. In the center is a small spit of a fire. Sparks fly out like shooting stars.

Annie leads her boyos into the crowded tavern. She floats more than walks to the center of the room.

"Who-op! Hello the camp!" she hails the room. Her pearls

sparkle like a string of stars. But them pearls ain't near as bright as her smile. "I'm here to tell you true, I rode a lightning storm down the Milky Way to come here this very night. Moment I touched down, I snared the swampiest gator and gave his hide a real rub-a-dub. And I sure can whip every man in this sorry, good-for-nothing place!"

Coby and Cody stand to at the entrance, holding their pistols ready.

"Who-op!" Cam dances a one-legged jiggity jig, moving to the middle of the room next to his mam. Crow and Chance stay armed and ready as they circle the room looking into each and every face there. Ain't a one that holds their eye.

Just then Tiger roars, a bellowing, thundering shake that brings them all to their feet. That's when I walk inside the circle. He follows me in and roars again. Now them men jump to, wild with fear. They can't get to the door, so they press against the wall, flat as flapjacks.

Annie chuckles, placing her hands on her hips. "Howdy, little River. 'Bout time you showed up," says she.

Tiger jumps atop one of them long tables and stretches full out. He yawns, his black lips curling over his large canines. Don't you know, he's all smiles now, them teeth gleaming like Annie's pearls. His tail thumps the table in delight.

I decide it's my turn. "Who-op!" I sashay around the room. Just like Da, I look each man in the eye. "Ain't it true, I'm the daughter of that old snapping turtle himself, the king of the river! I was raised on the Big Muddy and cut my teeth on a paddle. So here I am, you rough-and-tumbles. I outshine the Carolina moon, outdance a streak of lightning, and when I have a mind to, I outsing them Kaintuck wolves!"

And with that, I bring that fancy fiddle up under my chin and show them how it's done.

I play a fast reel. I see them men tapping their toes, but they're still shooting wary glances at Tiger. They ain't moving off the wall.

Annie crows. Cam continues his jiggity jig.

And just that moment a new voice raises up, a booming voice, deep as the rock of ages. From out of them shadows, a man walks up. He's not near as tall as Annie and her boyos, but he's a real bear, true enough. He's got as much hair on his chin as on his head, and there ain't taming either one.

"Who-op! Who's that wee chickabiddy?" Ain't none of us need an introduction. Don't I know him, true enough, that rapscallion who thought he could beat Da.

It's Mike Fink.

Chapter Thirty-Six

Annie puffs on her cigar. She squares off with Mike Fink, elbow planted firmly on the table.

Ain't I seen this story before? A stream of sorrow drifts through me as I remember the last time I saw Da.

Tiger sleeps right where he lies on that long table. Ain't no one sitting with him except Gurdy, whose face is in a worm of worry as he watches Mike Fink. Maybe he's remembering Da, too. Or maybe he knows Mike Fink's a regular curly wolf with a hair trigger of a temper.

Cam and Crow sit nearby watching their ma. The other boyos stand at their posts. Cully is swapping howdies with a keeler, while Cody's watching a card game unfold.

Another time there might be a bloody rough-and-tumble between Mike and Annie. But now they sit here in this ramshackle tavern, each smiling pretty.

"Followed some rumors that I'd see an old friend here. Might be some treasure buried in these parts," says Mike Fink, blowing smoke rings with his cigar. Nervous whispers pass through the tavern. Without losing his hold on Annie's grip, he leans in real close. "You ain't heard these same rumors?"

"Sure I did." Annie smiles. I know that smile. She gave it to Da just as she twisted her wrist to wrestle him down. "These are interesting times, Mr. Fink."

"Especially when you have codfish pirates like Laffite and half the rabble in New Orleans looking for your pretty head," says Mike Fink.

Just like that, she slams Mike Fink's arm down hard enough to make the table tremble. "You hunting me, too?"

"You found me, remember?" His smile turns crooked.

"I wouldn't have found you if you ain't wanted to be found." Annie returns the smile.

I snort. Annie shoots me a prickly look, but I've had enough of their twaddle.

"Laffite is a scoundrel," I say. "Mother Colby is the scum on his shoes. They plan to lord over the Mississip like a couple of goosey cowards. You rather have one of them, or them British, or them Spanish dandies telling you how to boat down our river?"

There's rustling at the tables as keelers and flatters and woodsmen now look to me. Ain't no one telling me to hush up.

Gurdy clears his throat. He's nodding, even smiling.

And I say, "I for one don't need some highborn telling me my place! Ain't that the truth of Da?"

The tavern goes quiet. Mike Fink loses his crooked smile. Even Annie Christmas takes in a sharp breath.

"Well, go on, little River," she says. "You speak your mind on this. Don't let us stop you!"

"This here chickabiddy got a strong whoop. A real fighter by the tail," Mike Fink snorts.

"Da wouldn't go down without a fight." I sit mightily tall now. "He wouldn't just hand the Mississip over to the likes of them dandies. He'd give them all a good hiding. Ain't no one knew the river like my da, and he gave that knowledge to me. I know when she's fitified and when she's woeful. I know when she's plum cracked. But it don't matter how she flows; this here big river lets us make our own place."

Mike Fink leans forward, chomping on his cigar. His eyes, blue as a clear sky, are giving me an eagle's glare. I lean forward and glare straight back.

"Your da was some," says Mike. "I see his grit in you, girlie. But while there's truth in your words, why should we listen to a pip?"

"Well, there you are and there you ain't," I say. Reaching inside my boot, I bring out a gold piece. It sparkles in the dim light as I lay it on the table.

Mike whistles, dropping his cigar. Others stand up to gaze at the piece.

"You listen because we got the goods," Annie says. "There's treasure to be had, sure enough. Goes all the way to Blackbeard, and before. And we're going after it."

"I heard tales about you and Dan Fillian partnering up. If them tales were true, I knew something big was going on." Mike Fink howls. He's eyeing that piece of treasure with the same stare as a hungry bear. "You still ain't said why you're here."

"Here it is, then." Annie puffs a giant circle. "Laffite is on our tails, and bounty hunters are after our heads. We need the biggest thundering brigade we can pull together, and no one thunders louder than you—except for me, of course."

"Well." Mike puffs his cigar, and then he gives a thundering laugh. "Why ain't you say something afore all this yammering?"

Don't you know it, that very night a new brigade forms. Mike Fink calls us the Tiger Brigade. This here big river ain't ever seen the likes of us, not even when Da was king of the river.

But he's smiling proud, my da. I just know it.

Chapter Thirty-Seven

All day the three-boat flotilla follows the current. I take my spyglass, which Chance fixed better than new, and look across the big river. There's a storm in the distance. Lightning dances across the horizon in some silent reel, but our brigade is slowgoing.

The *Big River's Daughter* reaches the sharp point of a bend. Annie heads her into the current. The boyos fight heap aplenty to reach the other side of the river.

If it ain't sharp bends, it's woolly sandbars.

"Stand to!" Annie booms. Chance and Crow, Cully and Cam, and all the boyos stand with poles ready. "Heave there, my loves! Keep moving, keep moving, boyos!"

Finally they push us over the sandbar.

"Stand to!" Mike Fink booms as his keelers follow us around the bend, and when that big river opens up, the wind in our favor, it's a race.

"Who-op!" Mike Fink stands on his bow. He salutes Annie Christmas as he flies by.

But there ain't no beating Annie. She crows, and Cully checks the rigging on the sail, and the *Big River's Daughter* flies with the wind.

As dark edges the horizon each boat bears toward land, lines ready to tie up for the night.

Before the sun wakes up, the *Big River's Daughter* takes the lead and floats to Baton Rouge. That place is a pitiable collection of shanties. I can stand on one side of the town and spit to the other, just like that. But this shantytown is the hub for surrounding plantations, and plantations mean money. And don't I know, we're needing heap a plenty goods where we are going.

Before we leave the docks, however, there's a sad chore to be done.

Annie's boyos start taking that shiny keeler apart, plank by plank.

I know how it goes. Where we're going, she can't go. Most keelers pull apart their boats every time they moor, only to walk back upriver and rebuild for another float down.

But this here *Big River's Daughter*, she was some, all right. Something shinier, something special. Ain't it a shame to see her torn apart.

"Don't you worry none, little River," says Annie. She's woeful at the sight, too. I see it plain enough in the tear that rolls down her cheek. "It's us that makes her home. As long as we got family—you, me, and my boyos—we got her. Don't you worry none. We'll rebuild her, bigger and shinier. You'll see, true enough."

"Ahoy the boat!" shouts a familiar voice. I look about. Don't I know that dandy well enough! But this dandy ain't no codfish. Tall and oak-straight, he's dressed in gray, with a hat near as tall as himself. He waves a cane at me. "I've been expecting you, Miss River. Mighty glad to see you again."

Himself a plantation owner, Spencer's one to take advantage of the big river. But he ain't ever took advantage of Da. Spencer is one of the few planters Da called friend.

"I heard tales of an orange-headed lass and her pet roaming the river's woods." Spencer speaks with a heavy English lilt, more a song than talk. "So I say to Mrs. Spencer, that has to be our Miss River. No one has orange hair but Fillian himself!" His smile straightens, and he gives me a nod. "My sincerest condolences, Miss River. The world is a much darker place with your da gone. We shall miss him terribly. For now, come along. We have much to discuss."

I ain't sure Da is dead, I want to say. But I think that I'm the only one that still carries that hope.

Mike Fink holds back suddenly. He looks to me, then to Annie, then to Spencer.

"So, Spencer," he says, his eyes narrowing like a snake's eyes. He's holding the hilt of his pistol like he's going to draw. His keelers come in close. Mike's grin turns dangerous.

"I know you to be a friend of Dan Fillian," he says. "That makes you a step above most, I say. But you're still a planter, you prettified codfish."

"Not that kind of planter." Annie smiles, slapping Mike's shoulder. "Lead on, Spencer. I believe we have business to discuss!"

"What do you mean, not *that* kind of planter?" Mike settles his pistol in his belt. "There's more than one kind?"

Annie slaps him again, harder. Mike Fink near pops his whistle.

"Spencer is one of Da's *investors*," I explain.

"I told you, me and Dan Fillian had a plan. So let's go talk things over." Annie moves to slap his shoulder again, but this time Mike Fink swerves about.

"A plan, you say?" Mike Fink is as confused as a wayward eddy. He looks to me. "You know about this, do you?"

I grin my grinniest and give him a nod.

The big house is surrounded by cypress and live oak. It's been a long while since I sat at such a fine table. I didn't sit so still then, but I'm doing my best here. At least this time I ain't bound by a dress that looks like worm food.

Tiger sits behind me, chewing on a turkey. He's smiling, all right, and *brrr*ing in delight. There ain't no slaves on this plantation, just survivors of the great earthquake. Like them we saved in that river town, they had no place, so they came here. There's hands aplenty to tend the fields, but that's done so they can eat. The real work and the real money on Spencer's plantation come from his river trading.

He and Da had a good deal going. Da lorded over the river, bringing particular goods to Spencer to trade. Spencer found a way to move the goods to them who paid premium prices. Da had trading stations all the way up the Mississip, spreading to the Ohio, and some into Canada. Spencer even had plans to outfit everyone who went west.

"Drink up, my friends!" he sings. Like the rest of us, he ain't one to pass up possibility, either. "This here peach brandy comes from my finest orchard. And this is a new concoction I'm quite proud of: ginger beer."

I ain't ever tasted such a delight as the ginger beer. It tastes so sweet, like it's dancing a jig going down.

"And you, Miss River, I see you still carry your da's spy case," Spencer says. "Your da carved that and made the spyglass while he was staying with me, a long time past. He told me he found that wood in old Mexico. He told me it was an ancient tree, a tree that fire and rain couldn't destroy—that is, not until the Spanish chopped it down. I see you gave it a new fitting; you've taken good care of it."

Annie wags her head, a curl of cigar smoke wrapping about it. She's wearing a familiar smile, the same one she shared with Da that night in the blockhouse. I know she's thinking of Da. "That old river pirate. He's been dogging after that treasure since he first came to the river, and I never knew."

Spencer studies the handle on the spyglass and smiles in recognition. "I see he's leading to the Big Bayou. That piece of land is No-Man's-Land. No one goes there but the very stink of humanity. And orange-headed lassies with their orange-striped kitties."

"That's where we'll find Harpe," I say. I know that is the truth of it.

Spencer nods, smiling all the more. Just like Da, he ain't one to pass up possibility. "Well then, it would seem the Fillian and Spencer partnership continues with some new opportunity. Let us drink to our success!"

Now a partner in the Tiger Brigade, Spencer loads us up with supplies and gives us more men. We're fully packed and raring to go. There's a boodle of us marching through the bayou. I slog through the shallow water, dark and thick with lily pads. Cypress trees swallow us whole. Swamp swallows swoop in and out of the hollows, and black vines twist through branches, tree to tree, like thick black snakes. Some droop so low, Cully ducks so as not to hang himself.

"Hold to!" Gurdy points to one of them vines. Suddenly, it writhes about and drops into the water, slithering into the dark tangle.

Cully winces. "I hate snakes."

"They seem to love you well enough," Cam hoots.

Annie Christmas and Mike Fink look ahead and behind. All the boyos walk quiet, looking about, armed and ready.

We ain't alone.

There are biting flies bigger than bees swarming about our heads. There's a granddaddy snapping turtle watching us from between the knees of an old cypress. It snaps its huge horned beak and dives below the surface. There are coon and possum aplenty, and black squirrels barking from the treetops. There are gators, too, eyeing us before they disappear in a swirl of bubbles and ripples.

But that's not who I'm talking about when I say we ain't alone.

Da told me about the time he come to this fearsome place, long before he knew Ma. Running away from his old ways, he came to these parts as a tenderfoot. He met Annie Christmas here, her string of pearls not so big then. He met Gurdy here, too.

Them other keelers think it a mockingbird calling out, or a puma, or some owl. But Gurdy looks at me and winks. He knows who's watching. This Big Bayou is full of people running away from something: refugees from the revolts, slaves on the run. Other men, like my da, running away from old lives. Ain't one of them will be found unless they want to be.

And for them who watch, here's what they see: me and Gurdy and Tiger walking together. They see Annie Christmas and Mike Fink walking together. Don't they know, ain't nothing brings these two together excepting some new calamity. And it's a-coming.

Chapter Thirty-Eight

The earth heaves up and turns dry. The canebrakes grow some thirty feet high, with stalks as thick as Gurdy's arms, choking out every green thing. Most of these keelers ain't used to such closed spaces. They're all jumpy as mice with a cat on the hunt. Even Tiger snarls. He knows them canebrakes offer good hiding for all heaps of trouble.

Gurdy takes the lead, using Big Sally to cut a path. The brigade weaves a single file through the bush.

Except Tiger. He moves where he wants. He ain't one for staying put and soon disappears into the tangle. And then I hear it: something grunts. Tiger ain't alone in there!

"Tiger?" I shout.

Gurdy holds me back, his grip like iron. I fight him, twisting every which way, but I can't get loose.

"River!" Annie shouts from behind. Just like that, Cully grips me by the shoulder.

"You can't go after him!" he says.

I wiggle like some worm trying to get free. "He ain't wild as you think. He can't fight!"

"He's good, River." He shakes me, like I'm some rag toy, until I can barely stand. "You done right by him. Trust in that! Just like how your da trusted in you."

Tiger roars, raw with rage. All around, birds spew out of the tangle, and something yowls. There's a bloody rough-and-tumble going on in that canebrake. The cane trembles with the fierceness of it. But it ain't trembling near as much as I am.

"Bear," Gurdy whispers.

"Tiger can't fight no bear!" I shout.

Right then it goes stone quiet. And it's quiet for a long, long while.

"Don't have to hold me so tight," I hiss at Cully. But he tightens his grip anyway as we hear more yowling.

"That don't sound like a bear."

Everyone stands still listening to Tiger's roaring, when a dog howls.

Gurdy says, "It's a tracking dog!"

"Tiger!" I lunge forward, breaking Cully's grip on me, and make a mad dash toward the noise.

"River!" Gurdy roars himself. But I'm loose now, and they can't catch me. The cane whips across my arms as I run, then I burst into a small clearing. A black bear huddles in one corner, roaring and swatting at Tiger. Its haunches bleed where Tiger's claws raked through its meat.

In another corner, Tiger crouches, his tail whipping mad.

There stands a third beast in the clearing. It's a barrel of a dog, as round as that bear, as tall as that cat, and ugly as sin. It aims to take on both the bear and the tiger. It snarls as loud as the big cat roars.

"Tiger," I whisper.

The dog whips its head about, snarling at me, tensing its haunches. It's attacking, all right! It's attacking me!

But then Tiger steps in front of me, his lips pulled back in a deep, fearsome snarl.

The bear whimpers. It knows if Tiger and the dog fight, it can escape. It's inching back into the cane, getting out of their way.

Then, something sings by my ear. I see a flash of metal, and the dog wails. Its haunches swing out from under it with such force, the beast flops over. Big Sally is stuck deep in its hind leg.

The bear shoots off as Gurdy steps up. He looks to me, to Tiger, then to the dog.

He says, "I know better to tell the sun stop shining or the river stop running than to tell you to stay put. But, girl, one day you fall into something so terrible, you no get away in one piece!"

"We done well enough." I scratch Tiger's ears. "I ain't left his side these many weeks. Couldn't do it now. That's not what friends do."

Gurdy tugs at my ear. "No, it ain't."

"I was looking hard for that bear, too!" Right then, a man steps out of the cane into the circle. He's bald as the full moon. He wears a red bandana, the same red as Gurdy's. He walks up to that ugly dog, and it whines, tries to stand, and stumbles. The man looks at the wound, shaking his head. Holding the dog down, he pulls out Big Sally in one easy move. The dog squeals like a babe. Don't I feel sorry for it now.

The man looks to Gurdy.

"That my best dog." He flips Big Sally about, holding the tip of it, and offers the hilt back to Gurdy. He takes the bandana off and wraps it about the dog's leg. "You well, brother?"

Gurdy's brother? I look to Gurdy, confused.

"So I am," says Gurdy, taking Big Sally.

This man then heaves that ugly dog over both his shoulders. The dog whimpers with the tossle but settles comfortable. Then this man looks to me. "Do she look like her da! But your da, he no like cats."

The battle between the beasts is forgot. That's how fast change comes on the big river. It seems that's how fast it moves in the Big Bayou, too.

"How long it be, brother?" says this man.

"Last time, as I recall, you had more hair," says Gurdy.

"You, too, way back then," says this man. "I hear tales of a river whelp and some pet. Know I find you soon enough. No think harm come here to my best dog. Thought you like dogs, Gurdy?"

"No knowing it yours, Girard. Thought it might hurt River."

"She not one for minding her place, is she?"

"Not hardly," says Gurdy. "Sorry about your dog."

"He too ugly to die just yet." This man Girard smiles.

Chapter Thirty-Nine

Seems like when Da came across them two, way back then, Gurdy took to the river, while Girard took to the bayou. They ain't seen each other since. But the way them two carry on, it seems like no time at all passed between then and now.

Girard leads all of us through the canebrake. The ugly dog whimpers, but there it hangs on Girard's shoulders like a sack of flour. Mike Fink yodels, his voice bouncing off the clouds. He's singing to an old march: "Through the woods I gooo, And through the bogs and mire . . . And to my heart's dee-sire, Oh, diddle, lully daayyy!"

The dog whines, and Gurdy winces. Annie rolls her eyes. But I join the tune, and don't we make a fine time of it. "Oh, diddle, lully daayyy, Odee, little lee-ooo-day!"

Now Tiger roars like he's singing, too. More join in as we roll along.

Finally the canebrakes fall away. Live oaks hold up a cloudy sky. We reach a split-log cabin with a mighty porch, one big enough to dance on.

Girard carries his dog inside and lays him by the hearth. Annie and Mike, Gurdy, too, all follow him in. But I stay on that porch, easing next to Tiger. He stretches full out, ears all a-twitch as he takes in every noise. The rest of them river rats set up fires across the clearing. There they wait.

I wait, too, but I don't know why. I listen to them talking inside.

"Strange new faces roam the bayou," says Girard. "Been

hearing about a whole brigade of slavers making their way inland."

Gurdy whistles so hard, Tiger and I stretch up. I look inside the door at those sitting round the table.

"Slavers," says Gurdy. "And pirates. And bounty hunters. Girl, come away from the door now. Show him your da's spy case."

I snort and walk in. I lay down my gold coin. I say, "This here coin belongs to my da. How special is it?"

Girard looks at the gold coin, nodding his head. His frown deepens. There's something telling in his look. There's something different about this coin. He scratches its surface. Then rolling it between his fingers, he bites it. "This here doubloon from Dan Fillian, this be some bad juju."

Girard sits quiet, quiet as death itself. Then he rises and sets the table with tankards and rum. He's the first to drink, taking a big swallow. He wipes the rum from his lips.

"See this doubloon, this here cross on the side? This be old, old gold. No seen the likes of this for three hundred years. As the story go, Moctezuma bring Cortez into the heart of his Aztec Empire. Called the big city Tenochtitlan way back then. He think this man Cortez be some sort of god. But Moctezuma, he be a clever king and want to learn all about Cortez. Know the enemy, he think. So he bring gold to the Spanish warrior, and he bring silver. But it only made Cortez more gold hungry. Cortez held the emperor hostage as his conquerors burned through the city, hunting down all its gold and silver. They took every last bit, all the gold and silver that had been passed down king to king since the Aztecs' beginning. Them Spanish melted it down and stamped it with their own mark. This here, that their mark.

"Word got out about the treasure he found. More Spanish come, wanting to put down Cortez. Cortez barely escaped with his life. He left that old city and all his treasure. When he come back some time later, the empire was dead. Moctezuma was dead. The treasure was gone. So Cortez built up a new city, called it Mexico City. But all that gold, it ain't been seen since.

Some say Spanish found it a hundred year later and sent it to the new king of Spain. But before the ship was long out of port, Blackbeard attacked and plundered that gold, adding it to his own cache. At least, that be the story as I heard it."

Mike Fink snorts. "If the story's true and Blackbeard got his hands on the treasure of the Aztec, then Mason found Blackbeard's cache. Little Harpe kills him for this heap plenty gold."

Annie whistles in awe. "This be the biggest treasure in the history of treasure." Now Annie Christmas looks to me. "Your da, when he came down this way all those years ago, he found Little Harpe. Maybe he made a deal with that devil Harpe to split the treasure."

"He told me, this will show me the way." I nod. "But if Da knew about it, why ain't he take the whole of it, not two pieces? Why'd he stay on the big river?"

Gurdy leans forward, shaking his own head. "Maybe he saw no need for the treasure. He got all he want: your ma, you, and that big river. He just waiting for the right time to do something big with it." He nods to Annie.

"To back our plan to build up the trade routes along the river, and out west." Annie chuckles. "So that's why we hunt down Harpe. We'll convince him to help us."

Girard wags his head. "Ah, brother, and here I thought you come home for my good cooking."

Gurdy laughs, too, and leans forward. "You take us through the Big Bayou? There some big storm coming, brother. That earth quaking no so bad as what ahead of us. This here gold, it be our way out of it, true enough."

Girard looks to Mike and Annie, all holding his stare. He looks to Gurdy, who's looking to me. Then Girard looks to me, too.

"You some pip," he says. "Look what you gather here. Ain't nothing like this brigade ever sweep through the bayou. Ain't you afeared? This here Big Bayou be in the middle of hell itself."

"My da got us all here, and I aim to see this through. I seen what happens when the earth trembles. It don't scare me no more. Don't matter about them goosely cowards Laffite and the war coming. I ain't backing down ever again."

"Well now." Girard slaps his brother's shoulders. Gurdy winks at me. "Can't have no pip stand taller than me—now, can I?"

I'm right behind you always, says Da.

Chapter Forty

Gurdy and Girard walk together, brothers in arms. They lead the way into the stand, a shameful rickety of a hut where highwaymen and pirates come to trade. I ain't leaving Gurdy's side, and Tiger ain't leaving mine. So Gurdy gives up trying to put us in our place.

It's near as dark inside as the outside when we arrive. There are few rushlights burning, and the fire pit is just aglimmer. It smells full of wet swamp and smoke.

Tiger strolls up to some tables, sniffing the food. He takes a half-eaten chicken. Like mice, them rogues scatter across the room, out of his way.

All but one. There's a shabby old man sitting by himself, wearing some hangdog look. His hair falls in greasy strands across his face. He looks near to starving, but he ain't touching his chicken. He don't see Gurdy and Girard step up to him or sit across from him. He don't lift his head up till Tiger sits next to him, sniffing his plate. Only then does the old greasy man look up.

"Thought you hanged eight years afore," Gurdy says.

"You have me confused with someone else, friend," he growls. Then he turns to me and smiles. There's something astir in that smile: this one's mean as a twisted snake.

"Heard tell you fought with the British." I aim to stomp on that snake before he slithers off. "That you, Little Harpe? Turncoat?"

"Ain't you some fresh peach." He grins. There's a gap

between his front teeth so big, a river could run through it. "You got me confused with someone else."

"Heard tell"—I grin my grinniest best—"you killed your own children."

The old man leans forward, coming in real close to me. Gurdy leans forward, too, bringing out Big Sally.

The man looks to Gurdy, then back to me, sucking through his teeth with a hiss. "I killed many peoples, peach. I killed many chillun in my day. So you be careful."

"You ain't scary." I lay my hand on Tiger's shoulders. Tiger snorts, and then he yawns, showing them big teeth of his. He licks his chops, too. "Now, that's scary. You a broken old dog use to think himself a wolf. You killed everyone got in your way, even your family. And here you are, running for your life. You ain't no wolf after all."

"Peach, you got a mouth—"

Gurdy twists Big Sally. "Took us a while to hunt you down. You no stay in any place for too long. That tell me you afeared of something mightily powerful. Someone on your tail, true, true. That why your spine be all in a twist?"

"You think them Brits, them Frenchies and Spanish, even them cracked American weasels scare me?" Now Harpe, greasy old bear, wags his head. He laughs, but it's one of them fearsome cackles. He holds his hand up. I can see it clear in the rushlight: Three fingers are gone right down to the nub. The remaining two are mangled. His hand looks like a claw. The deep, gashing scar snakes down his arm. With that arm he shoves his plate toward Tiger. Chicken bones fly.

"Sure I do," I say. "Da told me once, pirates fear water because they see the faces of all their murdered innocents looking up from the watery depths. They fear those innocents will rise up and pull them under if they get too close. Bet you see them faces everywhere. I bet you afeared of your own shadow."

The old man stiffens, his eyes narrow to mere slits, like he's seeing something familiar.

"I know you," he growls. "That orange hair. You the pip of

Dan Fillian, that thieving, rantankerous varmint!" He bolts from his bench, lunging at me with his clawed, mangled hands, but Girard holds him down. Harpe kicks and kicks so hard, the table topples. Tiger jumps to his feet with such a roar, the other rogues scramble out of the stand like mice.

Annie and Mike now walk into the hall to see what the fuss is all about.

"You hold still, you pig fart!" Mike grabs him. With one great heave he slams Harpe into the wooden bench, and the old man calms.

"I had it, Blackbeard's treasure!" Harpe mutters, near to tears. There ain't a place on him that's not all atremble. "It's mine and he stole it! All these years I been looking for it."

"He's tetched with gold fever, Ma." Cully chuckles. "He's got it bad."

"Enough of this prattle," Mike huffs. "What are you talking about?"

"I had it. A man could live ten lifetimes and never see the like of it. I got it from Mason. But the French were closing in; I was trapped. I couldn't move it by myself, so I needed another body to help me. I thought Dan Fillian just another orange-hair highborn, an easy dupe. And once he done what I needed him to do, I thought him an easy kill. But he said the French and Spanish wouldn't stop looking. Once word spread about who had it, others come looking, too! So he came up with a plan to hide it real good. He carved a fancified map so we could come back when it was safe. And to keep us both honest, he carved a key to the map. He kept the map; I got the key. So we took off: he went up the river, and I went down the Natchez Trace. It worked; we got the French off my tail. But it's my treasure. I ain't going to share it with some scallawag, so I went back. And that varmint done took it! He had moved it from our hidey-hole. Like some ghost, it just disappeared. Bounty hunters been dogging me about it—and I don't even know where it is!"

Mike and Annie, and all the boyos in the room, turn toward me.

"Da ain't got it!" I bring out the spy case.

"That's it! That's the map!" Harpe fumbles as he reaches inside a coat pocket. With the toothiest smile he pulls out a long leather pouch and pours coins of silver and gold onto the table. I look at them, turning pieces over. Some have marks on them just like mine. It's a river of shiny, like stars in the rushlight. And then he pulls out a long tube. Annie takes it from him, turning it over in her hands, examining the carvings.

"Can I see your glass, River?" With a smile she holds out her hand. "Don't worry none. I'll take good care of it. Cam, Crow, clear the room of anyone that don't belong to us. Keep them away from the windows. Cully, bring me a torch."

As Cully gathers more rush to bound up a torch Annie pulls apart Da's spyglass. Then she looks inside the cylinder.

"Your da was some fancy carver." Using her knife, she scrapes the inside of the cylinder, then blows inside to clear away her shavings. Holding the tube up to the light, she winks at me. "See?"

The torchlight shines through Da's carvings, casting the map on the wall.

"That's well and good, Ma," says Cully. "But it's just a map of No-Man's-Land."

"Keep your britches on, boyo." Annie smiles all the more, outshining the pearls around her neck. Taking Harpe's tube, she scrapes a layer of reed out of the inside. Then she twists it to fit inside the spyglass and holds it up to the light. The map on the wall changes as the two carvings merge. In the middle of the carving, in what looks like a big lake, is a boodle of islands. There, too, even my fancified letter *R* takes a new shape: the scrolling tip points to one island.

Annie nods at me and shakes me gentle. "That old pirate could see around every bend in the river."

"I know that place," Harpe whispers, his mangled claw shaking as he points to the letter. "It's a speck of an island in the middle of Big Lake. That's where that villain buried my treasure?"

"That whole land be wretched evil." Gurdy shakes his head. "My people stay away from it for good reason."

"Heard tell Laffite hides out there," Cully says.

"Sounds like the perfect place for a visit, boyos!" Annie hoots. "Let's get packing."

Just then Tiger growls full of menace. Outside, shots ring out, and Cam and Crow and others rush inside the stand.

"We got company!" Crow warns as he loads his musket.

Cully douses the torch. More shots are fired as Annie and Mike draw their pistols and cock them. Girard looks out the window.

"Close ranks!" Annie shouts to the keelers and runaways. "On guard!"

Even them rogues stand close to the hut, pistols and knives drawn, muskets and cutlasses up. They look to the trees, to the shadows beyond. Ain't nothing puts the fright in a man more than knowing death is stalking you.

"Give us Harpe!" a voice calls out of them woods. Can't tell how many are hiding there. "Do that, and we'll let the rest of you go!" Even before the echo of them words quiets, the rogues in front of the stand scatter to the winds.

"If all they want is you"—Annie looks to Harpe—"maybe we should just give you over and be done with it."

Just then the air comes alive with the crackles of gunshot as the men fire on the stand. I can hear the moans of the fallen, and others scuttle about looking for cover. We drop to the floor, covering our heads. I put my hand on Tiger, trying to keep him calm. I can feel his muscles tense, like he's getting ready to bolt. His tail whips behind him.

"You in the woods!" Crow shouts. "Ain't you heard? That old cracked jack is dead."

"No, he ain't," the voice shouts back. "But *you* might be if'n you don't hand him over!"

"Seems like you going to shoot us anyway!" Crow laughs. But it's a sinister, makeready laugh. He nods to his brothers Cody and Coby, who start crawling across the floor. Annie points to Cully and Cay, too, who join them as they head toward the back, slipping outside into the woods. Crow shouts to the newcomers in the woods. "So, friend, you sure you want to take on this bear? Sounds like you got more bark than bite!"

"We got plenty bite!" the man in the woods shouts back. "Come out here and we'll be mightily glad to show you just how sharp our teeth can be!"

Just then Mike shouts so loud, the timbers shiver. "You got something to do, do it. If not, take your leave!"

"Mike Fink, is that you?"

"It depends on whose asking," Mike shouts back.

"Well now, ain't this one happifying surprise." The voice chuckles. "You wouldn't be in the charming company of Annie Christmas now, would you? The bounty on Harpe, dead or alive, is well enough, but boy, howdy! Them pirates Laffite is paying some mightily handsome for that group."

"And here I thought we were friends," Crow shouts back.

"Well, there's friends and then there's money."

Annie speaks up now, a thundering roar. "You found us, true enough. But finding us and taking us down are two different things!" And she shoots into the woods. Someone screams as she hits her mark. Others in the hut take her lead and fire.

The strangers fire back.

"If you get shot," Cully whispers to Crow as he reloads his musket, "can I have your share? I've had my eye on this piece of land up north."

"I ain't dead yet." Crow reloads his pistol, pulling back the hammer.

"Nope, but you look all corpsified." Cully winks at me.

"You two quit jawing." Annie glares at her sons. "Something ain't right. What's taking your brothers so long? They should have them by now."

I look out the window, plucking out several burly figures moving to surround us.

"Of course something ain't right," Mike Fink huffs. "If all was right, we'd not be stuck in this pit surrounded by them sheep in wolves' clothing!"

Another shot rings out, followed by a long dead quiet.

Finally Crow shouts, "You in the woods?" But no one answers, and he turns to Annie.

Suddenly a scream cuts through the woods, a hair-raising, bloodcurdling howl that sets Harpe to whimpering and Tiger, ears lying flat against his head, to growling. Another shot's fired.

"You boyos answer me here and now!" Annie shouts. "Or I'll come tan your hide but good!"

"All's well, Ma," Cody calls out. "We got 'em! But one got away."

Just then Cody and his brothers walk out of the woods dragging in tow four bounty hunters. They stumble buck naked, their legs bound by their own britches and their hands secured by their own shirts. We clear out of the hut to meet them, Tiger running the fastest and taking to the woods, glad to be free.

"We got more problems, Mam." Cody grabs the greasy hair of his captive, turning the face toward Annie. The man's eyes are swollen near shut, his nose bent and bloodied. But I recognize him all the same. So does Cam.

"That man belongs to Mother Colby," he says.

"Our man is fast." The man smiles through the blood. "He'll report what happened here to Mother Colby and Laffite, and ain't no place safe for none of you! Word's out now!"

"Leave them in the hut. Use some rope to make sure they can't get away," says Annie. "Let's move out."

Chapter Forty-One

We move quick as Girard leads the way through the Big Bayou. This here land is the middle of hell itself, a muddle of shallow waters that creep around a tangle of low islands. Sometimes the water opens up and deepens all at once. A man walking unawares can disappear under the surface just that fast. And there's all manner of creatures slithering and crawling in this wild tangle.

Gurdy and Girard walk with sticks, poking through the muddle of wet grass, rolling earth, and floating tangle. Mightily careful, I step where they step. The swamp bubbles and oozes, and it stinks like rot.

"Smells like Curt's bean soup." Gurdy snorts.

I chance a laugh and suck in a deep breath, tasting the rot. "Yep, tastes like Curt's bean soup."

The earth trembles, and I near fall on my knees. My stomach jumps right up to my throat. We slog across the floating earth, careful of them gators and snakes and giant fish and leeches, all living in the tangle and fallen logs. Like Da told me, pirates have a strange fear about water. That Harpe is so cracked, he's whining every time he puts his foot down.

Tiger yowls. He ain't liking this swampy muddle, either. He stays close, his tail hanging low.

None too soon, the earth hardens into a clump of a small island, and with the land beneath me, I finally get my footing. I start running through a huckleberry thicket right into a patch of cypress forest. Tiger, Gurdy, Girard, and Cully run by my side.

And just that quick the earth falls away as the water tangle returns.

One of Mike Fink's mannies screams as he drops through the tangle. Before any might jump to and pull him out, a log rolls over. The surface bubbles as the gator does him in.

"Gator!" Someone booms a warning. Another log slides quick across the tangle, disappearing under the green rush.

"Find higher ground!" Annie crows.

Now Harpe yowls, his fear of that gator chasing off what's left of his sense. He shoots off, scrambling for the dry land but instead falls into the water. His arms flail like mice whiskers. The water splashes as another gator hits the water, chasing him down.

Crow and Chance jump after that old man. Cam pulls him out as Chance shoots the gator.

Annie shakes him back to his senses. "You crazy coot! Try that again, or get one of my own killed, and I'll tan you alive!" Harpe sputters water and black foam, swamp-water rot dripping from his clothes.

"Land ho!" Girard crows, pointing up to higher ground.

Tiger ain't waiting for anyone. He dashes ahead, and I'm right on his tail.

At long last we get out of them dark waters and set up camp. Annie's boyos take turns standing guard, full armed and ready. Others march the perimeter of the camp, and them not on guard huddle close to a fire. Some sleep. But most just lie there listening to the swamp. River rats know the swamp wakes up at night. Something's always slithering or skittering, hooting or howling.

Chapter Forty-Two

As Gurdy stews up a squirrel Harpe sits close to the fire, not bothered by the smoke. He's still stinking like swamp. Only flies and skeeters have courage enough to get close to him.

"I ain't killed Sam Mason," Harpe says. He sucks a breath through his gap. "I killed heap plenty people, sure enough. But I ain't killed him. The French caught up with us in Missouri. They were shipping us to New Orleans when we worked out a plan of escape. But there was a shootout. It was them Frenchies that shot him—weren't me. But I took his head, and got away, and turned it in for the bounty. A thousand dollars goes a long way. He owed me, sure enough." He looks to me with a crooked smile. "That Mason was a Virginny highborn, a hero of the War of Independence, just like your da. He surely thought himself some. He called me a traitor, too, peach. But I showed him, didn't I? Turns out, he weren't so different from me. He blamed them all—them American, them Spanish, them Frenchies, all of them—for killing his family. He killed as many women and men, sold as many slaves as ever I did. When we first met, he was living in the cave in the rocks overhanging the big river. One night we got ourselves some rum and had a good ole time. That's when he told me about his treasure."

"Why he tell you?" Annie asks. "You ain't kin. From what I hear, Mason weren't no pickle brain."

"Rum makes friends out of enemies just that quick." Harpe smiles.

Mike Fink hoots. "This is quite a story. Heard tell they hanged you with a man called May."

"You think I'm pickled?" Harpe chuckles. "Told you that bounty come in handy. I paid my way out. They hung some other poor mannie. I went to Mason's hidey-hole. I found it right where he said it was. It's more than you can imagine. Gold and silver and every sparkly that there be. Well, not too long after that, I met your da."

I nod, fingering the spy case. Ain't seem hardly true, this big story about Da and the treasure and Little Harpe. "So my da, he knew this murdering excuse for a pig."

"It don't surprise me none." Annie chuckles. "Them were dark days for your da. He disappeared for weeks, months even, between sightings. No telling where he went off to, and he didn't talk about it when he came up for air. He just come back into life, talked like he ain't been gone at all. Earned himself quite the reputation, too. There's always a high price for freedom, little River." Annie looks to her boyos. There's Cully, smiling pretty. Cam is laughing loud as can be, and them twins Cody and Coby are a-chuckling. There's Crow, always alert, watching the swamp. Then says she, a shadow of sorrow covering her smile, "Always a high price, true enough. But most days, ain't it some."

Suddenly, Annie crows so loud, all heads turn in her direction.

"Who-op! You hear me, you swampy beasts. I once fought a duel with a thunderbolt and walked away without a singe!"

"Ain't you some, Annie Christmas." Mike Fink yodels so loud, the night screeches back. "You be a real square-rigged craft! You call the dog with the best of them. But here's a tale from the long ago. It got so cold, even the sun froze, got itself stuck between two mountains. Well, I was heading home after a good day's hunt when I come across this sad, cold sun. It was plum wore-out, feeling a bit unappreciated, you see. Well, I ain't got time for pitying, I say. It took a couple of good kicks, but don't you know it, I sent that sun back high in the sky."

166

"You a real man of heart." Annie whoops as loud as she might.

But right then, just as quick as any wind off the river, Gurdy whistles. Annie and Mike turn sharp about, taken by surprise. Now Gurdy says, "You some, you two river folk. But this here the Big Bayou, and we got our own tales. My Mee-Mee says, there be a snake. No so big a snake, but no so small. It give our people the frights to have a snake living so near. But everything be full of soul, says Mee-Mee, so our people let it be. But that snake begin to grow. The more it grow, the more it eat. The more it eat, the more it grow. It grow so big, it stretch from swamp to valley and back again. And it so mightily hungry, one day it turn on them people. The people no choice but to fight. It some fierce battle. Many die fighting, until there be one left, the last one standing. He no back down, neither. He give that snake some final blow. It be one good blow, and the snake be done for, but it take many a day to die. It twist and turn and coil in its death struggle. And with every move it dig away the earth, until there be a mighty cavern. That cavern fill with water. And that be the Big Bayou."

Now Girard chuckles. "Brother, you home now."

And don't you know it, I bring out that fancified fiddle. I stir up a soaring melody, burning up my strings, near as spicy as Gurdy's stew.

And them boyos, they hoot and they holler. Cully flashes his pretty teeth, taking Cam by the arm. They do a fast reel, and some others join the circle. For a tick in time it's life back to normal, wild and woolly.

I look out there in them swampy shadows. Mother Colby and the pirates Laffite have gone into cohoots.

And I play a little louder and stomp a little harder, hoping to chase my trembles away.

Chapter Forty-Three

The sun struggles through the morning fog. It's as weary as us marching through it. Seems like Mike Fink needs to give that tired old sun another good kick.

Tiger's full of menace, his tail whipping about. He holds his head up, smelling the air, ears all a-twitch. He's warning me about something. That big cat is so tetchy, ain't no one but me dare walk close to him. Not even Gurdy.

I rest my hand on Tiger's shoulders. He begins to trot. Something's astir. I should have seen it coming with all this fog around us.

"Hel-lo the camp!" Gurdy yodels.

"Hel-lo! Hel-loooo the camp!" Girard hoots.

From out of the trees, some hoot back. More gather about, walking out of log homes with no walls, roofs thatched with palmetto leaves. It's a camp easily torn down when the need comes. In the center there's a big pot of gumbo bubbling over a fire. It smells like Gurdy's stew, and my stomach growls with hunger. There's gator smoking on a spit.

A man comes out of the biggest house, himself tall as one of them oaks. He's some, all right. His hair is tied back in long braids, in a red bandana like Girard's and Gurdy's. He wears the slave's clothes, cotton breeches and white shirt. He also wears a brand on his cheek. But he don't walk like no slave.

He steps lively, coming to Girard with arms wide open. They embrace and slap each other's back.

"Vincent." Gurdy gives him a nod. But he keeps to my side.

"Glad to see you, brother," says Vincent, offering him a hand. "Looks like you lost your crown there?"

Gurdy combs his hair. "Growing old, I guess."

Mike Fink chuckles. Vincent turns to him and his mannies. Mike loses his chuckle under the wary stare. They eye each other, but they keep their pretty smiles. They puff themselves up like two mountains. I'm thinking, there's about to be a bloody rough-and-tumble.

Ain't that always the way of it?

Annie Christmas comes up, stepping between them two. Ain't no one ever bests Annie Christmas. Her smile outsparkles them both. She slaps Mike heavy on his shoulder, so heavy he spits out his hot air. I think he spits out a loose tooth, too. Vincent laughs, but Annie crows and slaps him, too. He heaves out his hot air. She yodels, louder than them all, "This one's good!"

That's when Vincent sees me. And Tiger. He looses his smile, just that quick.

"Howdy," I say.

Now Gurdy chuckles. "You no afeared of some kitty cat, brother?"

Tiger stretches and yawns. Vincent jumps back a full three strides.

I lay my hand on Tiger's head. Tiger sits with a snort.

Now another steps out of the big house. This old woman floats across the ground dressed in white cotton, her hair as white as her skirt. But she wears a red bandana, too, wrapped around her white hair. This is Mee-Mee, don't I know it.

"Boyos! You behave now! This be a good day, a good day! Gurdy come home!"

She's all smiles as she comes to Gurdy, arms wide open.

"Mee-Maw." Gurdy smiles, too. He's near to tears as he takes her in one big bear hug. He holds her a long, long moment, one so long seems like a life's come and gone. As he lets her go he points to me. Mee-Mee lays a hand over her heart.

"Look at that orange hair." She chuckles. "Just like your

poppy. I seen you once, you know. You no remember." She walks right up to me and stoops down to see me eye to eye. "You no bigger than my hand, way back then. Your poppy a good, smart man, but no so smart about babies. Especially little girl babies. For a while, he live on nothing but pure hope. But he do good, I say. That the last time I see you. Last time I see my Gurdy, too." Mee-Mee stands up. "I think you both do good."

She turns to Tiger. Tiger *brrrs* in a snarl and licks his lips. She smiles and pats that big cat. Says she, "You some fierce kitty; behave yourself."

There's some on the watch, marching the perimeters. They yodel a greeting to Gurdy and Girard and wave in our direction. Girard hoots back.

But more gather round us. They watch Mike Fink and his keelers, Annie and her boyos. They keep a distance from me and Tiger, but they're a-smiling and nodding. And they talk all at once about what they seen and heard.

"This be dangerous time," says Mee-Mee. "The British, the Spanish, the Americans, them planters. Pirates. They all hunt these parts again. It all we can do to stay out of their way. Bad times now. Bad, bad times."

"You no run forever," says Gurdy.

"This from a boy who run away from home? You think your Mee-Mee don't know what you been up to? Your Mee-Mee knows everything," says Mee-Mee. She looks to Annie. "You think this man Harpe and his gold change all this?"

Annie wags her head slow. "Some gold ain't changing nothing. Every day more come and take away our river, drain your swamps for their own farms. They keep pushing us to the edge of the earth, and then they take that, too. We keep running away; we keep hiding; but either way, they keep taking."

Mee-Mee says, "Hiding keeps us living."

Girard says, "Running keeps us living."

Annie says, "But not for long. Maybe now we stand up. Maybe this here's the time we quit running."

"I don't remember Da ever running from no one. And I ain't seen you running much," I say.

"I'm running, little River," says Annie. "Just not as fast as others. Laffite has it out for all of us. But your da, he saw all this coming. They called him king of the river for good reason."

"You say we make war on them?" Mee-Mee asks. "We got enough war, child. There enough killing."

"No war, no killing, Mee-Mee." Annie smiles. "This here is business."

Mee-Mee straightens her back with a hoot. She slaps her knee, then slaps Girard's knee. With two hoots now, she turns just that quick to slap Gurdy's knee. Gurdy twists about, out of his Mee-Mee's reach.

"Mee-Mee?" he says. "You think this funny?"

"I think she bright as the North Star," says Mee-Mee. "She say, use that gold to buy them out. She say, use that gold and build us a business so big, they no hold us down. Then we got them but good."

Gurdy and Girard and all them men look to Annie.

Now Annie says, "We had ourselves a plan, me and Tenderfoot. We come up with it way back then. We been working and planning, and putting it in place ever since. Mee-Mee be right." Annie leans forward. She smiles so pretty, ain't no one looking away. "Dan Fillian had investors like that Spencer every turn of the way. We use the gold to buy them out."

"What if they don't want to be bought out?"

"Then we make them partners."

Mike Fink slaps old Harpe against his shoulder. "Ain't this a glory!"

The old man coughs. He's still watching the trees.

Tiger's ears are twitching, his tail thumping. He's watching a feller run up to Girard. Girard leans in close as the man whispers in his ear.

Girard leans over to Mee-Mee, and whispers in her ear. I can tell by the way she wags her head, it ain't good news.

Girard leans over to Gurdy. After a moment he looks to Annie. She waves to her boyos to be quiet.

The quiet sweeps through everyone. All of them move in close.

"You better move quick, what you planning," says Gurdy. "Laffite just sail up the Deep River. He be in the Big Lake in the next few days. He's setting up his own business."

Part Four

December 1812

The storm comes to the Big Bayou. Da said, life is full of possible imaginations. And ain't this the biggest one! It's us river rats and runaways, us rough-and-tumbles, taking on them biggeties in their fancified suits.

Ain't no way of knowing how many are dogging us, and the men sleep uneasy on account of what's coming.

Except that Mike Fink. Cam, too. They sleep well enough. Harpe, he's more cracked than ever.

We don't stay still for long. Annie Christmas keeps us in tow, rushing forward to the Big Lake. That pirate Laffite is anchored there, and we're going to meet him head-on.

There's a storming coming, true enough, and it's us. Them pirates Laffite know it.

Chapter Forty-Four

Laffite's schooner drops anchor offshore. He has sailed through that narrow pass just beyond the Gulf of Mexico with a master's hand. That pirate had to know every which way the current flowed, how the winds blew, and how the sands shifted so as not to run aground in the shallows.

Ain't she some, with two masts touching the clouds. Her narrow hull is built for speed. She's fast and smooth, like a tiger on the hunt. Ain't no ship faster than that one, I bet.

Using Da's spyglass, I spot the pirate patroon pacing across the upper deck. He's dressed in fine trousers and a waistcoat, his wide-brim hat hanging low over his forehead. He looks just as prettified as the day he came for me at the Sure Enuf. He's even swinging his cane like a king's scepter. He's bellowing something to the men below, who scramble like rats. Next to him stands that ox of a man Dominque You.

And next to him are them twin dandies Alaire and Alain.

"Lookee there." I give the glass to Annie. "It's them bamboozling codfish."

"That's not all." She points to the shoreline, returning the glass to me.

I turn the spyglass to shore and see three skiffs beached on the sand. I inhale, watching Hogg Tyler barking orders to other rogues gathering there.

"Looks like he brought his whole brigade with him, including Mother Colby's bilge rats," I say.

"Makes sense." Annie nods. "Laffite ain't stupid. You said

yourself, he knew me and your da were partnering in a new business. Laffite may not have believed any tales about the treasure, but no self-respecting pirate can ignore rumors about Annie Christmas and Dan Fillion's whelp and Mike Fink, and even Harpe himself, come together. That's just too big to ignore. Mark my words, he's waiting for us."

"What about the treasure?" I pack the spyglass into its case. "Which island is it?"

Harpe's clawed hand, all atremble, points past a line of islands to a speck a mile off the shore, just on the other side of the pirate's schooner. "It's that one."

"Ain't this a joyful situation?" Mike smiles, and it ain't one of joy. "Don't think Laffite will be all that gentlemanly if we ask him to move aside for a bit."

"Looks like I need to get on that boat and ask him politely," says Annie with one of her prettified smiles. But it's that same smile she gives just before she wrestles the enemy down.

"You think Hogg is going to just hand over them skiffs so you can talk to his big boss?" Mike spits.

"I got an idea." Now I smile. "But you ain't going to like it none."

"Prolly not," say Annie and Gurdy together.

"You need to get on that boat," I say. "And you need them onshore to be looking somewhere else so he can't see you steal them skiffs. I can do that."

"You ain't going alone," Gurdy growls.

"I ain't." I nod toward Tiger, who's lying in the tall grass.

"And while this go on, I take the old man to the island to see what we can see," Girard says.

"Ain't that some." Mike chuckles. "We got ourselves a plan that might work. All right, then."

I ain't wasting any more time. Tiger jumps to my side, and we march down to the shore.

"Hel-lo the camp!" I roar loud as I might, standing just as tall and grinning my very best.

Every rogue swarming the shore turns my way. Even that

old sausage Hogg Tyler. He narrows his snake eyes on me and stomps forward like he's about to strike. But then Tiger grunts. Hogg Tyler stops dead in his tracks.

"Ain't it nice to meet old friends again?" I call. "Heard tell you looking for me?"

Tiger roars one of them fierce roars that's more teeth than bite.

"He's just playing." I pluck Tiger's ears. Tiger wags his head and sits. "He already ate his fill for the morning."

But Hogg Tyler ain't laughing.

"Hobgoblin." He draws his pistol. He's looking to the woods, knowing I ain't alone. "I promised you we'd cross paths again. You've growed up a bit since last we met."

"Ain't you the man of your word, then." I grin all the more.

Just then Mike Fink oozes out of the shadows behind me.

"Don't believe I had the pleasure of your acquaintance," he booms, rocking on his heels.

Hogg Tyler looks to Tiger, to me, then to Mike Fink. "I heard of you, sure enough. Heard you might be in these parts. I was looking forward to our meeting." He's puffing himself up as his men slide in next to him.

Others step out of the trees as Mike's keelers and Gurdy's family of runaways join them.

The storm is landed. The calamity done hit the shore.

All eyes are on us now, away from Annie. I don't take my eyes off that Hogg Tyler. In the corner of my eye, I see Annie running with her boyos. They reach the skiffs and push two of them into the lake. Quick they begin to row toward the schooner.

Mike Fink crows as he jumps. And in that one giant, high-flying leap, he closes the distance between himself and that old sausage Hogg.

Hogg lowers his pistol on me. And with that wily grin he fires. But his aim is as crooked as his smile. It ain't me it hits, or Mike Fink.

I swerve about. Girard goes down, clutching his chest. Blood is spreading like a fast-flowing eddy.

Not far from him Harpe screeches, arms flailing. Hell's bells! He's done cracked, running away like a crazy man and back into the woods! All heads turn in his direction. Before Hogg and his rogues take up arms to shoot, Mike Fink, his keelers, and Mee-Mee's runaways charge the shore, waving their cutlasses and firing their pistols and muskets.

Gurdy, leading the charge, plows into one of Hogg's rogues. Them two roll over in a heap of growls and dirt.

Girard is down, but someone still has to get Harpe to the island. Ain't long enough for my heart to skip a beat. I just run.

I chase after Harpe. Tiger bolts ahead of me. The big cat swipes at the man's legs, sweeping them from under him. The old cracker tumbles with some fearsome shriek. I grab the old greasy by his collar, trying to force him to his feet. But he's too big. He writhes like a snake and I lose my hold.

"Why you running away, you cracked old fool?"

"No, no, no." He wags his head, his eyes rolling about funnylike. Standing before Big Lake, I bet he sees all them he murdered, more ghosts than fish, all waiting to pull him under. He's cracked all the way through. "Won't go there. Can't swim. Won't swim. Not in there."

Da was right smart to hide the treasure on that island, knowing this grizzled old Harpe won't dare cross the water to get to it.

Tiger's running to the shore, ahead of us.

"Get you up now! This ain't the time for silliness!" I pull harder at the old man, at his beard, at his hair. His hair is too oily and I can't get a good grip, or I might yank out the whole of it.

I glance at the tumble behind me and see Hogg reaching for his belt, grabbing for his blade. He aims to stick Mike Fink. But that Mike Fink, he's got the fists to back the tall talk. Even before Hogg brings his blade up, Mike clocks him across the chin. Hogg spins about in a fancy reel and falls to his knees with a thud. The keelers and runaways sweep by like a rogue wave. I look for Gurdy, but I can't see him.

Don't I know it true enough: It's all on me now. I have to

get this cracked old codger to the island. Then once Annie and her boyos take over Laffite's ship, we load the treasure on it and ride the wind.

Off in the water two skiffs creep close to the pirate's ship. On one prow, Annie stoops, armed and ready. On the other, Cully stands alert, watching his mam. Chance and Cam, Crow, Cully, and Coffee row like a machine.

"We move out now, you goosey coward," I call. Only then does Harpe scramble to his feet. Taking his sleeve, I drag him to the shore, chattering like some lost child. He's cracked all the way through.

"Not the water, not the water!" Harpe whines.

"You old man"—I point to the island—"move fast. Your life depends on it." Harpe stumbles as he climbs into the last skiff on the shore.

I stow my fiddle on the boat's bottom but keep the spy case strapped tight to my back. Then I push off. Behind us the battle roils.

I hear it, but I don't look back.

When I can no longer touch the swampy bottom, I swim, pushing the boat ahead of me. Tiger swims next to me, ears flicking as he snorts water.

Harpe's already drowning in fear. He's bent over, hiding his face and holding his ears as tight as he can.

"You sit still!" I struggle to keep hold of my temper. "Eyes forward! Keep to the plan!"

I keep swimming toward the island, pushing that boat. The boat sways and it's all I can do to hang on. Suddenly, Harpe squeals, and then the old fool stands up.

There's no keeping it steady. The more it rocks, the more Harpe shrieks. And suddenly, the boat rolls over, spilling its guts including my fiddle. Harpe's screaming and thrashing like a drowning chicken. His kick cracks my chest, knocking the wind out of me, and I spiral to the swampy bottom.

I push myself up and finally break the surface. My chest hurts as if a mule kicked me square.

"Swim, you cracked son of a gun!" I grab that old bear, dragging him along like a potato sack.

I kick as hard as I can, pushing our way through the water.

It's like that day again. I'm running as the blockhouse explodes, shaking the earth. I'm running away from the fire . . . running as the river turns backward . . . running . . .

Chapter Forty-Five

Finally I reach the island. I can hear Tiger in the trees ahead, and I follow his roar.

"No more! No more!" Harpe whines.

"Ain't that right, no more." I shake the old man's beard. "You crazy old man, you're a heap more trouble than an old skunk twisted in wire. This island ain't big enough to spit across. Now help me find this treasure."

"I'm dead, and I'm in hell, ain't I? And you're the devil himself," Harpe rasps. "I just too ornery to know the truth of it."

"We follow the plan," I declare. The anger wells up like some summer storm. All them on shore fight to give this man time to help me find the cache. "You move, or I let Tiger have you for lunch."

Harpe scrambles to his feet. At last we run.

It's just a tick in time, but I see the pirate Laffite's ship just off the island's shore. It's moved! Annie and her boys must have made it to the ship! But now, don't I know it, the real fight begins. Surely she and Laffite are at each other's throats.

That's when I catch a glimpse of another skiff on the shore. We ain't alone on the island.

Suddenly, the air explodes around us. The pirate ship is firing at the island, at us! Tiger jumps over a fallen log and swerves on a tick. Soon enough he's way ahead and out of sight.

Harpe wails all the more and flails like a wounded bird. He stumbles over the log, bringing us both down. No matter how fast we run, it ain't fast enough. I pull at Harpe's arm, trying to get him to his feet. His legs wobble like water.

I fight to keep my own legs under me. The very earth shakes beneath my feet. Suddenly, I'm shrieking as the earth opens up and swallows me whole.

And I'm falling . . . falling into blackness.

Chapter Forty-Six

It's dark. As my eyes adjust, I realize I'm in one mighty cavern. The only light drops from above where I fell through the earth.

"Tiger!" I shout. But only my echo shouts back, *Tiger!*

It hurts all over just to move, from my chest, where Harpe kicked me, to my legs and backside, which I landed on at the bottom of this pit. I fumble my way through the dark. It smells like brackish muck and wet earth. The air is thick with salt and lime. I can hear water dripping.

"Tiger?"

BOOM! BOOM! Cannon fire explodes the earth above me! The pirate's ship has opened up all its cannons on the island. But why fire on the island? Surely Annie knows we're here! Hell's bells, it sounds like an all-out war up there!

The earth shudders with each impact. It rains dirt and rock and bush and branches. I dive out of the way, choking on the dust and heaving with the smell. Suddenly, the hole above me opens up, letting light fall in sheets.

And that's when I see that the earth at my feet sparkles like falling stars.

Easing to one knee, I dust off the sparkles. Them stars are coins.

Silver coins.

Gold coins.

My eyes follow the light now, and I can make out them coins spread across the floor. There's more. Heap aplenty more!

There are cups fit for a king, pocked with red and green jewels.

There are crowns fit for a queen, and platters big enough to sleep on. There are statues of funny dragons and birds. There are spears and knives.

And there are pearls. Pearls rounder and bigger than them pearls of Annie Christmas! I reach for a string of them, fingering them shimmerings.

Ain't it the honest truth, this here is the lost treasure of them Aztec. Of that pirate Blackbeard, and of blackheart Mason. The treasure Da buried long ago.

Above, a shriek rips the air apart. It's Harpe, and I just know he's a goner.

Before I have the chance to blink, someone falls through the hole into the cave. At first I think it Harpe, but the figure stands up taller than tall. I skitter as far into the dark as I can. Like a rat escaping the light, I flatten myself against the cave wall, trying to get smaller, and feel water running down my back.

I turn and see water cascading down. And where I stand, the water rises—so high that coins swirl around my ankles. But don't you know it, they're swirling by me quick, as if they follow a current! I think it's more than a spring. I think the cannon fire opened up a real river!

I look up, and standing in the water is the pirate slaver Jean Laffite.

His green eyes flashing, the pirate takes in all the sparkling treasures. I stand stone-still, so still it hurts.

But it's too late.

"Ah, petite River!" He smiles wicked. "Do you not think I saw you swimming to this island? I'd say it's a pleasure to see you again, but we both know that wouldn't be true."

"You killed Harpe," I whisper.

"Oui, of course." He nods. "And I killed your kitty cat, too."

"No, you ain't." My heart is about ready to jump through my chest. I swallow hard. "You ain't so prettified now. You just another bilge rat my da put in his place, just another lowest form of humanity."

My words hit their mark. Laffite lunges at me. I try jumping out of his way, but he's fast and grabs my shoulder.

"You want to see wrath?" He gnashes his teeth. "You are right; I made a fortune selling certain goods. But I just as easily dispose of those who are more trouble than profit." He clutches my throat, lifting me off my feet. He's leaning in so close, I can see the veins pulsing on his neck. "I squash insects like you every day and don't think twice about doing it!"

"Don't you know"—I struggle against his grip—"we river rats ain't so easily put down!" I pull both his ears so hard, I near rip them off his head.

Laffite yowls. But instead of loosening his hold, he lunges into it, slamming me into the wall so hard, the spy case rams into my back, snatching my last breath.

I can't scream, can't barely move. But I ain't done in yet. I claw at his eyes, drawing blood. I aim to pluck them out.

Now he drops me, stumbling backward.

The earth explodes with another cannonball. Rocks and earth rain down as the ceiling crumbles with the impact. The cave is collapsing atop us! And the current swirls up to my hips.

But I ain't going down just yet. I take a strong grip of Da's spy case. And then I scream, a ripsnorting shrill. I swing the case hard and fast, and clock Laffite. I hit him hard again, hard as I might—so hard, the case cracks.

I swerve about, knowing the current has to go somewhere. And anywhere is better than here.

"You ready, River?" Da asks.

Chin up, I nod and straighten my shoulders.

"Round to, then!" Da booms. "I'm right behind you always!"

I take a deep breath, dive under, and swim like a fish born in the river. . . .

I follow the current into the dark.

Chapter Forty-Seven

⚓

The last light flickers soft on the big river. There's an osprey floating on the wind.

"That's Ma"—Da points to the light—"easing us home. And that big ol' bird, see how he plays on the wind, following the light!"

Then Da sings to me about home on the Mississip . . .

"Da?" I wheeze. My chest burns for want of air.

"Seems like I'm always pulling you out of the river." Annie Christmas smiles. Them pearls about her neck sparkle like stars in the night sky. I feel her hand on my shoulder, hauling me back to my senses.

I'm alive. I'm on dry land. I'm on the shore where the battle took place.

I sit up, my ears ringing like church bells. The sun shines high, and I blink at the brightness.

And that's when I hear the quiet.

Quiet like an afternoon on the river that lost its flow.

Quiet like when a battle's done.

I look to Annie. Her smile ain't so bright now. Don't I know that grieving look well enough.

She gives me a slow nod, and a tear escapes. Says she, "Don't you know, there's time aplenty for tears. Right now we got to move. Laffite's escaped. He's gone for help, and he'll find it easy enough in this no-man's-land. He's got crew all over." She looks at me and winks. "He's a bit riled that we took his ship."

"Gurdy?" I'm all ashiver with wet and cold.

"Little River." Gurdy rushes up now. He's gathered coats and dry clothes. "You safe now." I slip my arms around his neck and hold on tight.

"River." Cully eases next to me. He's lost his smile, too. And now I can see why.

Cam and Chance are lying on the shore. Cody and Coby, them twin suns, lie in stillness next to them.

Crow and Coffee stand guard while Cay and Cane stand near their ma. There's more bodies everywhere.

Mike Fink watches the lake. Anchored just off the shore, Laffite's ship rests easy now. Annie Christmas won the ship, but at a heavy price.

I look to the island. It's tore up plenty. Fire sweeps across clumps of trees, black smoke coiling and drifting on the breeze.

"Laffite was on the island." Suddenly, I stiffen, loosing my hold on Gurdy. He sets me down, and I struggle to get my legs under me. "Tiger?"

I try jumping to, but my legs wobble like pudding. I can't get them to work. "Tiger! He's on the island!"

"River!" Gurdy takes my head and turns it inland. Tiger stands atop a log, far from the water. "Seem that big cat just as stubborn as you. 'Twas Tiger that found you in the water. He no left your side. You no remember? That big cat swim better than you!" says Gurdy.

Tiger sees me, true enough. He roars and trots my way, circles me once like he's giving me a big hug. He rubs his ears against my shivery legs, and I go down in a tumble, wrapping my arms about his neck.

Ain't that some.

"I saw the treasure." I cough the words.

"We know." Anne smiles soft. "Seems like you got your own pearls! You were clinging to these when I pulled you out of the drink." She holds up a small string of pearls. Them ain't so fine as hers, but they're treasure, true enough.

With the island on fire, there's no way to get back for the rest. I lost it. Cam and Chance, Girard—all them keelers lying still on the shore—they died for nothing?

Tears rise up inside me, too strong to stop the flow. I shake my head slow, tightening my hold on Tiger.

"You there!" Mike Fink booms, turning to me. "You done with your blathering? Can we get back to business now?"

"That underground river spit out more than just you." Annie points. "That treasure, it's all over the bottom of the lake!"

Chapter Forty-Eight

There you are and there you ain't. We got our treasure, sure enough. But this ain't a prettified story, and there ain't a prettified ending, at least none that you expect. But that's life on the raggedy edge, and change comes on the wind.

Laffite escaped the island the same as I did. He's fitified about losing his fastest ship. Because them pirates were slavers, losing such a ship set back their business. Besides, he can't let Fillian's hobgoblin beat him, so Laffite called for all-out war against us river rats. Ain't no one more wrathy than some vexed pirate think he's lost his due. When he finished licking his wounds, he swooped down on the Big Bayou with an army of men, aiming to kill all who helped us, including Mee-Mee and the rest of Gurdy's family. He aimed to clear out that bayou and make it fully his own.

So Annie Christmas and the rest of us came up with a new plan. We'd lead the runaways from the Big Bayou up north and give them bits of the treasure to set up a new home. Until the time comes when they can go back again.

Annie promised Mee-Mee they'd all be safe.

On the first run Gurdy leads Mee-Maw and her family. Annie and some of her boyos lead another group. Cully and me and Tiger, we take another group. Them pirates can't follow all of us all at once, no matter how many men Laffite gets. But he don't catch us. Sometimes we go across land. Sometimes we sail in Laffite's ship. Ain't it true justice that we rename the ship *Big River's Daughter*! That a ship that once brought them in chains now takes Mee-Mee and her family to freedom! All along the way we have men like Spencer and other "investors" who hide us.

So we continue to take the runaways north, some to Boston and some to Philadelphia. Some to as far away as Canada. It's a new plan, a big plan, freeing all them slaves. But we build ourselves a real empire. Da would like it, don't I know.

When we finish the run, we meet up with the brigade in Freetown. There ain't many of us left, not since that bloody rough-and-tumble on the shore of the Big Lake. There's Annie Christmas, with her string of pearls ashining bright, moving like a swan across the room. Annie's boyos stay beside her. But Mike Fink ain't here. He'd had enough of them pirates and their twaddle, he said, and off he went. I expect there's more to that story, but he didn't say.

These are still dangerous times. Laffite ain't the only one who wages war. The war in the Northeast against the British finds its way down the big river, right down to New Orleans. Laffite joins forces with Old Hickory Jackson, and they beat the British back to where they come from. Laffite is a hero now. But that just makes him more dangerous. He never forgot his defeat on the Big Lake. He ain't forgiving that we took his best ship and all that treasure. He ain't forgiving me.

But Annie Christmas don't scare easy. And don't she know the best way to bring her enemy down: the more slaves Laffite brings into the big city, the more times we go to New Orleans and take them north to freedom.

When we can't sail the ship anymore, we break it down and send the bell to Laffite. Surely that gets his goat! But try as he might, he can't catch us.

Now we make our way back to Freetown, Cully and me. That's when we hear the news.

Annie Christmas is dead.

And that's a powerful sorrow, so powerful I'm drowning in them words like the river run backward again.

There's a heap plenty stories about how she died. One story

says it was because a man finally beat her. Don't you believe it none. Ain't no one beats Annie Christmas.

Some say Annie charged into a burning flatboat to save a boodle of people. She rode the river like an angel and blew out that fire with a single breath. But the boat was sinking fast, and it created some powerful eddy. She went down with the boat, but not until she saved every poor soul on board. It's a grand story, true enough—so grand, I expect Annie told it herself.

But the truth of it ain't so grand. Crow turns pale as fire ash as he tells us. One day Annie felt pains creeping across her like a thousand marching ants. She felt so poorly, she went to sleep. And she ain't woke up.

As powerful as that sorrow running through me, it ain't near as mighty as the current sweeping through Annie's boyos. Ain't no one to pull them out but me. So don't you know it, I reach into that despair and tell them there's time aplenty for tears, but for now, we got to move! Then it's me who takes the helm of the *Big River's Daughter*!

And here's what I say to those boyos: "It's us that brings her home. As long as we got each other, we got her. Don't you worry none. This here brigade, we are the *Big River's Daughter*. We are as shiny as ever. You'll see, true enough. But for now, Annie Christmas made a promise, and it's up to us to see it through."

Epilogue

⚓

Cully hoots, pointing to the contraption coming down the Mississip. Black smoke roils like snakes out of two stalks as the steamboat chugs along.

"It's another one of them fancified paddleboats," Cully says. "It's getting mightily crowded on our Big River these days."

Tiger grunts. He's fully growed into them paws of his, walking easy as a slow-moving current. I count my blessings, he ain't felt the need to go off on his own. He's my family as much as Cully.

I expect Da would think him some, too, even if he didn't take to cats.

"True enough." I scratch around at Tiger's ears. He *brrrs*, rubbing his head about my legs. I say to Cully, "They done civilized our river, didn't they?"

"Oncle put some bounty on you." Catiche walks up from behind. Turns out, Catiche didn't take to her plaçage very well. It weren't a match made in heaven, shall we say. She heard tales about others finding their way north, heard it was me and the boyos of Annie Christmas taking them. Like so many others, Catiche ran off, hoping for a new life. I obliged her, of course. I don't turn down anyone who asks for help. And ain't it a red feather in my cap that I took her away under that pirate's watch! "You're a regular outlaw," Catiche says. "It's a wonder to him why no one turned you in as yet. It riles him something fierce." She tightens the bundle against her back. She's a bit taller now, and her dress ain't a prettified field of flowers dressed in lace; it's a plain cotton shift. And underneath, ain't it the truth, she's wearing britches and boots! Her hair, once aflow down her back, is coiled in a tight bun and covered with a wide-brim hat. We even call her by a new name, Cat. She smiles with the sound of it. Says Cat, "Oncle curses the day you came into his life. He said you changed his luck, brought him nothing but shame and bad business. He aims to tan your hide but good someday."

"Ain't you heard, Cat?" Cully walks up, showing his pearly whites. "Ain't no one beats River."

"And you, Cully, you're a huckleberry above my persimmon." I grin my grinniest best, touching my own string of shiny pearls. "Laffite ain't the first one to try, and he surely won't be the last."

"Maybe not, but ain't he the stubbornest bull?" says Cully. "Now he's got a burr in his britches something powerful. From what I hear, he's in another pickle with the governor. Might be a good time for us to move on. Heard tell that Mike Fink found himself a gold mine in them Rocky Mountains. Maybe we think about going out west, seeing what's in store there?"

I take out my glass, the one Gurdy carved anew for me. I take a sweep across the river, watching the steamboat disappear around a bend. "It's a thought. It surely gives us something to talk about when we meet up with the boyos. But until then, we finish what your mam started."

"It'll be good to see everyone," says Cully. "Heard tell Crow got himself a wife."

"A wife, you say." I smile. "Won't be long before we got a full brigade again! Looks like we in for some real fiddlin' when we get back to Freetown." I move my new fancy fiddle against my back, making sure it's secure.

"Enough twaddle." Gurdy snorts. "We have a march ahead of us. Best get moving."

"What do you think about going out west, Gurdy?"

"I hear plenty." Gurdy smiles. "It a place of possible imaginations."

The folk gather their belongings as we break camp. Besides

Cat, there's a boodle of women and children. It's slow-moving with this many running north. We keep on the ready, watching the woods, watching the river. We don't stay in any one place for too long. That's how we keep them safe.

Just then a pip cries out, angry that he was woken before he's ready.

"Don't you worry none," his mother coos, bouncing him against her back. "We almost there."

"Hold on, you chickabiddy," and I whoop. The pip stops crying and gives me a moon-eyed stare. "Who's this, you say? Why it's me, River Fillian, just so you know! You'll be telling this story to your children and to your children's children, so I'll make it a good one! I can outfight and outscream any critter in creation. This here story is all true, as near as I recollect. It ain't a prettified tale. Life as a river rat is stomping hard, don't I know it. It's life wild and woolly, a real rough-and-tumble. But like Da said, life on the big river is full of possible imaginations!"

I keep telling my story as Tiger takes the lead into the woods. The people fall in single file behind me as Cully and Gurdy take up the rear, armed and ready. I expect Annie Christmas is smiling pretty at the sight of us. Her and Da, true enough.

I'm right behind you, always!

"Who-op!"

Author's Notes

Annie Christmas: Annie is one of the first original heroines in African American folklore. Her tales were a favorite of the Creoles (people of mixed Spanish, French, and African ancestry) and American blacks in pre–Civil War southern Louisiana and the Mississippi River region. In fact, as with many tall-tale figures, there may have been a real Annie Christmas who inspired the tales.

Catiche: Born Catherine Villars (or Villard), Catiche—a common nickname for Catherine at the time—was the younger sister of Marie Louise. According to some scholars, Catiche was not made placée to Jean Laffite, and so was not entitled to economic privileges, but nonetheless she was made mistress to the pirate at a young age and bore him his only son, Jean Pierre Laffite. Not long after, Jean abandoned Catiche when he left New Orleans. Their son died during the yellow fever epidemic in 1832. Catiche remained in New Orleans and lived on for several more years, marrying the wealthy Pierre Roup of Santo Domingo. She died in 1858. Of course, in my story, Catiche dares to make a different choice.

Jean Laffite: Thought to have been born in 1776; his early life is a mystery. Some say he was born in France; others say in Santo Domingo. Much of the confusion may be attributed to the pirate himself, as he often told different stories, depending on who was listening. By 1805, however, he and his brother Pierre were firmly planted in New Orleans businesses and high society. Considered the last of the Gulf Coast pirates, he liked to call himself a corsair or a privateer, challenging anyone who dared say otherwise to a duel. At one point, he ruled a fleet of fifty sailing vessels. His buccaneers plundered mostly Spanish ships for anything of value: furniture, silks, crinolines and embroideries, dinnerware, wines and cheeses, even medicines. He was also a notorious slaver. In 1814 he and Pierre became heroes in the Battle of New Orleans, the last battle of the War of 1812, in which they defended the city against the British navy. For their efforts the Laffite brothers were granted a full pardon for their piracy. However, the city had seized Jean Laffite's ships and warehouse compound at Barataria and put them up for auction. Laffite was angry, demanding his goods to be returned. In 1817, feeling betrayed by the city and country he helped defend, Jean Laffite left New Orleans, never to return. Of course, that's not the end of his story.

Little Harpe: Born Wiley "Little" Harpe, he and his older brother, Micajah "Big" Harpe, murdered over forty men, women, and children, including their own families, along the Mississippi River and Natchez Trace. Historians consider them the first true American serial killers. He was an associate of another feared highwayman, Samuel Mason. Captured in 1803, Little Harpe was hanged in 1804—unless, of course, he found a way to escape.

Madame Rochon: Born in 1767, Rosette Rochon was the daughter of shipbuilder Pierre Rochon and his enslaved consort, Marianne. When Rosette became of age, she was made placée to Monsieur Hardy, and lived in Santo Domingo. During the Haitian Revolution, Rosette escaped to New Orleans, where she became the placée of wealthy New Orleans businessman Joseph Forstal and then of Charles Populus. Intelligent and astute, Rosette became a shrewd and successful businesswoman. One of her business partners was Jean Laffite. She died in 1863.

Marie Louise Villars (or Villard): A free woman of color, Marie was the placée of Pierre Laffite. During their fifteen-year relationship Marie bore Pierre seven children. Before the birth of their last child, Pierre abandoned Marie and the children. Eventually Marie married a wealthy Creole man and lived in New Orleans until her death in 1833.

Mike Fink: Like many folklore figures, Mike Fink was an actual person. Called the king of the keelboaters, he was known for his sense of humor as well as his willingness to fight. Once the Mississippi River became civilized with the introduction of the steamboat, Mike Fink moved out west, where he had many more adventures roaming the Rocky Mountains. According to some, he was a member of Ashley's Hundred, where he kept company with famous mountaineers and explorers Kit Carson, Jim Bridger, and Jedediah Smith as they searched for the source of the Missouri River. He died in 1823.

New Madrid earthquakes: Beginning December 16, 1811, and ending in late April 1812, a series of earthquakes shook the Mississippi River basin. Three of the two thousand tremors would have been measured magnitude 8.0 on the modern-day Richter scale, while six others would have measured between 7.0 and 7.5. Centered on the Mississippi River town of New Madrid, then part of the Louisiana Territory, the quakes were felt as far away as Boston, New York, and Canada. Entire river islands and towns disappeared, lakes were created, and for a short time the mighty Mississippi River ran backward. Sand blows, in which cones were formed by the eruption of sand onto the surface, can still be seen in fields. To this day minor earthquakes occur in this region. Scientists agree that it is only a matter of time before the New Madrid fault moves again.

Pierre Laffite: Born sometime before 1779, Pierre was the older brother of Jean Laffite. Known for his charm, Pierre was often the public face for the Laffite businesses. Although he was married, he entered a plaçage arrangement with Marie Louise Villars, with whom he had seven children. After fifteen years he returned Marie to her family and took Lucia Allen from Charleston as his mistress. He died in 1821.

Plaçage: In colonial New Orleans, as well as other French and Spanish colonies of the New World, plaçage was an accepted social practice for many wealthy white and Creole men, in which they set up a common-law household, similar to a common-law marriage, with a woman of color. The woman, called a placée, was "placed" when she was about fifteen, after being introduced to society in a very elegant affair called a quadroon ball, much like a debutante ball. The placée and her family received many economic benefits from the arrangement, including the legal transfer of wealth, ownership of property, and sometimes manumission, in which the enslaved family members were given their freedom. Usually, but not always, such arrangements lasted a lifetime, until the death of one of the partners.

Tiger: In 1806 a sea captain brought the first two tiger cubs to America. Sea merchants often brought baby animals that they had picked up during their travels: the first lion in 1720, the first ostrich in 1794, the first elephant in 1796, the first zebra in 1805. These animals, and many more, became part of traveling menageries and public spectacles. Between the years 1813 and 1834, according to scholars, at least forty-one animal menageries were traveling the U.S.

Underground Railroad: Many individuals and organizations helped fugitive slaves escape to the North and to Canada. According to one estimate, between 1810 and 1850 one hundred thousand fugitive slaves found their way to freedom. It was a long, dangerous journey, often taking many weeks and sometimes years to make. For example, in 1776 Harry, one of George Washington's slaves, escaped from Mount Vernon. He was evacuated to Nova Scotia in 1783, and was eventually relocated to Sierra Leone, West Africa, with his wife and three children. One organization in particular, the Quakers, had developed a methodical system to help runaway slaves as early as the eighteenth century. In 1786 George Washington complained about how the Quakers had helped his runaways. In 1831 the system was dubbed the Underground Railroad.

A note about the language: To help reflect a character's personality, I used many words specific to early Mississippi River life. This was a challenge because those were the days before the dictionary. People spelled words according to how they pronounced them and different pronunciations produced different spellings. To help me, I drew upon *The Crockett Almanacs*, a popular serial publication (1835–1856), which included many tall tales of life and adventure in the backwoods as well as on the river. I also used Walter Blair's *Mike Fink: King of the Mississippi Keelboatmen* (1933), which includes reprintings of Mike

Fink's stories as found in many nineteenth-century sources; Richard Dorson's *Davy Crockett: American Comic Legend* (1939); and Michael Allen's *Western Rivermen, 1763–1861: Ohio and Mississippi Boatmen and the Myth of the Alligator Horse* (1990), which explores the life and times—and tall-tale language—of the river men.

Wherever river men gathered, they told their tall tales. And, just as the storyteller was defiant and unruly, the tall-tale language defies the tidy, restrictive, uptight structure of formal grammar. It mocks it, in fact, often using pseudo-Latinate prefixes and suffixes to expand on the root. The result is a teetotaciously splendiferous reflection of a wild frontier life too big for mere words to capture. From these sources came such words as afeared, pollywog, honey-fogled and shecoonery, as well as many phrases and structures used in my story. I couldn't tame them either, so I tried to be consistent in my use of them.

River men used songs and calls to signal each other while working their many boats. Mark Twain's *Life on the Mississippi* highlights many of my favorite calls, like "Who-op!" which means "I'm here! Look at me!"

Want to know more?

Asbury, Herbert. *The French Quarter: An Informal History of the New Orleans Underworld*. New York: Thunder's Mouth Press, 1936.

Baldwin, Leland. *The Keelboat Age on Western Waters*. University of Pittsburgh Press, 1941.

Blair, Walter. *Mike Fink: King of the Mississippi Keelboatmen*. New York: Henry Holt, 1933.

Davis, William. *The Pirates Laffite: The Treacherous World of the Corsairs of the Gulf*. New York: Harvest Book/Harcourt, 2005.

Dorson, Richard. *America in Legend*. New York: Pantheon Books, 1973.

Feldman, Jay. *When the Mississippi Ran Backwards: Empire, Intrigue, Murder, and the New Madrid Earthquakes*. New York: Free Press/Simon & Schuster, 2005.

Hamilton, Virginia. *Her Stories: African American Folktales, Fairy Tales, and True Tales*. New York: Blue Sky Press/Scholastic, 1995.

Jagendorf, M.A. *Folk Stories of the South*. New York: Vanguard Press, 1972.

Sublette, Ned. *The World That Made New Orleans*. Chicago: Lawrence Hill Books, 2008.